—The—
Hidden
Jewel

Trailblazer Books

—The—
Hidden
Jewel

DAVE & NETA JACKSON

BETHANY HOUSE PUBLISHERS
MINNEAPOLIS, MINNESOTA 55438

Inside illustrations by Julian Jackson.
Cover design and illustration by Catherine Reishus McLaughlin.

Published by Bethany House Publishers
A Ministry of Bethany Fellowship, Inc.
6820 Auto Club Road, Minneapolis, Minnesota 55438

Printed in the United States of America

Library of Congress Cataloging-in-Publication Data

Jackson, Dave.
    The hidden jewel / Dave and Neta Jackson.
        p.   cm. — (Trailblazer books)
    Summary: While traveling in the south of India, fourteen-year-old
John and his mother encounter the Irish missionary Amy Carmichael
and find themselves drawn into helping the work of the Dohnavur
Fellowship.

    [1. Missionaries—Fiction. 2. Carmichael, Amy, 1867–1951—Fiction.
3. Dohnavur Fellowship—Fiction. India—Fiction. 5. Christian
life—Fiction.] I. Jackson, Neta. II. Title. III. Series.
PZ7.J132418Hi   1992
[Fic]—dc20   91-44062
ISBN 1–55661–245–1   CIP
                                                                        AC

This glimpse into the life of Amy Carmichael and Dohnavur Fellowship is based on the true story of an Indian girl named Muttammal, called "Jewel," and the young man, Arul Dasan. Many real people, events, and details have been worked into this simplified version of their story. However, the Knight family and the role they played are fiction.

DAVE AND NETA JACKSON are a husband/wife writing team who have authored or coauthored many books on marriage and family, the church, and relationships, including *On Fire for Christ: Stories from Martyrs Mirror*, the Pet Parables series, and the Caring Parent series.

They have two children: Julian, an art major and illustrator for the Trailblazer series, and Rachel, a high school student. They make their home in Evanston, Illinois, where they are active members of Reba Place Church.

CONTENTS

Chapter 1

Incident on the Cog Train

THE INDIAN SERVANT went first, loaded down with an assortment of baggage. Fourteen-year-old John Knight followed him out of the station, then stared at the strange train puffing at the edge of the platform. "Father!" he called back over his shoulder. "What kind of a train is this?

TRACK 2

It's so small—almost like a miniature train. And look!" John pointed. "The engine's on backward!"

John's mother and father emerged from the station doorway, each wearing a *topee*, or sun helmet, to protect themselves from the intense Indian sun. Sanford Knight smiled at his son's confusion. The tall English government official had only been in India for six months himself and understood how different everything must seem to his wife and son.

"This is a cog train," he said, "the only way to get up the steep hills to Ootacamund. The engine is placed at the back of the train so it can push the cars up the hills. And look between the tracks."

John squinted as he focused on the shiny tracks. A row of spikes ran like a third rail between them.

"A wheel beneath the engine grabs those cogs and helps pull the train. Now, come on, Leslie," he said to his wife. "In you go." Mr. Knight opened the door to the first-class car and assisted his wife into the train. Azim, their Indian servant, followed with the bags, stowing them in the overhead racks.

Laughter and girlish shouts caught John's attention. A flock of young Indian girls dressed in brightly colored long skirts were climbing into the third class car, along with a woman dressed in a pale blue *sari*. *That's strange,* he thought. *That woman looks English—or white, anyway. I wonder why she's wearing Indian clothing?*

The conductor, dressed in a blue coat and white turban, was calling "All aboard!" and the steam engine let out a mighty *whoosh*. There was a flurry of doors opening and people scrambling onto the cog train. John leaned an arm out the open window as the train jerked and made its way slowly out of the station. The Nilgiri hills rolled brown and dry on every side. His father said it was greener and cooler at Ooty—as Ootacamund was usually called—a resort town called a "hill station" nestled in the foothills of the Western Ghats.

The Knights were heading for Ooty to enroll John in the British school there. As the train lurched and groaned up the hills, he wondered what the school would be like. "All the English families come to Ooty for their holidays in the hot season," his father had explained. "It's a good place for a school. You'll feel right at home; the town is very British."

John wasn't sure he wanted to feel at home—not if that meant England. India was the most exciting place he had ever been. He and his mother had recently arrived from England to join his father, the new junior magistrate in the Tinnevelly District of south India. The senior magistrate was scheduled to retire in 1910, and the British government was giving his father one year of preparation to take over the civil duties of judge and magistrate.

From the moment John walked down the gangplank of the ship, India shouted adventure. Crowds of people swarmed in the streets, competing with bicycles, horse-and-buggies, and ox carts for the right of way. Donkeys loaded with bundles plodded slowly between village markets. Majestic banyan trees provided some shade and relief from the dry heat in

Palamcottah, the large town where the Tinnevelly District Court was located. Temple elephants paraded in the streets; monkeys scolded from the tall grasses in the countryside. John had been warned that sometimes leopards came down from the hills, though he hadn't seen any.

John sighed. Just the thought of entering the spit-and-polish corridors of an English boarding school, even if it was in India, was enough to bore him to tears. There was so much to see and do here.

Nevertheless, after a week of settling into their new home in Palamcottah, Sanford Knight decided they must get John into school without delay, and combine it with a short holiday in Ooty. They had already taken the regular train as far as it would go, traveling in the relative comfort of a first-class car with their Indian servant. The cog train was the last leg of their journey.

As John leaned on the window ledge, a movement toward the back of the train caught his eye. He leaned farther out. "I can't believe it!" he exclaimed. "There are people on the roof of the train!"

Mrs. Knight peered out the window and looked up. "Oh, my word. Someone could get hurt!"

Mr. Knight glanced up from the newspaper he was reading. "Mmm, yes. The lower castes are hopping a free ride. It's not legal, but tolerated."

Just then the cog train pitched as it rounded a curve, shaking the railroad cars severely. John glanced up just in time to see a poorly dressed Indian man slip and fall from the top of the train, landing soundlessly in the brush and rocks beside the tracks.

"Stop!" John yelled. "A man just fell from the top of the train!"

"Sanford, how do we stop the train?" cried Mrs. Knight. "He fell head first!"

Mr. Knight jumped up and pulled on the emergency brake chain. Nothing seemed to happen at first. "John!" Sanford Knight yelled, and John pulled on the chain with his father. A few moments later the cog train groaned and stopped, the steam engine belching smoke in protest. The Indian conductor came running to their car, obviously upset with John's father. "You stop the train? What is the matter, *sahib?*"

John pointed. "Back there! I saw him! A man fell off!"

The conductor turned and hurried back along the track. Other doors were opening in the other cars and people peered out. John scrambled after the conductor, with his father and mother following.

The train had gone several lengths beyond where the man had fallen. He was motionless and appeared to be unconscious. Dirty rags barely covered his gaunt body; he had no hat or turban. The conductor pushed aside the noisy crowd that was gathering and looked the man over closely; then he began waving and shouting at the other passengers in an unfamiliar language. It was obvious to John that he was telling everyone to get back on the train.

"What is it, conductor?" said John's father, who came up just then with Mrs. Knight and Azim.

"Nothing, nothing. We can do nothing. He is *pariah*—untouchable."

"I see," said Mr. Knight.

"What do you mean?" demanded Mrs. Knight. "We can't just leave an injured man lying beside the railroad tracks."

Mr. Knight pulled his wife aside. "Leslie, my dear, you don't understand. The Indian caste system is very complex—we mustn't interfere with their beliefs. Hindu religion, you know."

"I don't know!" protested John's mother. "But I do know that as a Christian and an Englishwoman, we must—"

"You are entirely right, madam," said a calm woman's voice. "Would you help me?"

To John's astonishment, the white woman in the pale blue sari walked right past the conductor and bent down beside the injured man. Her hands felt

14

over his body gently. "Nothing broken," she said. "But he has hit his head. We must get him into the train."

"Miss Carmichael!" protested the conductor. "It is not done!"

The woman ignored him. "Would you help me?" she said again, looking at the Knights.

John wasn't sure what was going on, but he liked the woman's gutsy attitude. "Yes, ma'am!" he grinned. His mother also stepped forward. Azim looked shocked and backed away. Reluctantly, Sanford Knight assisted his wife and son and the woman in the sari as they picked up the injured man and carefully placed him inside the third-class car. John tried to ignore the smell of the dirty body.

A loud cheer went up from the freeloaders on the roof of the train, and John waved to them in response.

Once back in their first-class compartment, John's father looked displeased. "I say, I will not have my wife and son getting involved in the messy little affairs among the Indian social classes. You cannot solve their problems with misguided sympathy. My job as an official of the British government is to rule and bring order to the country, while letting the natives take care of their own social affairs."

"Oh, Sanford," said his wife. "Don't look so dark. It was the Christian thing to do. We couldn't let the man die, could we? I wonder . . . who is that Carmichael woman?"

Mr. Knight sighed. "I have heard about her—a

troublemaker, they say. She is an Irish missionary, I am told, who refuses to follow the customary missionary methods. Instead she has gone about 'rescuing' girls, of all things, who belong to the temples, or something like that. All I know is that she has made a lot of Hindu holy men very angry."

"Don't those girls have families?" John asked, not understanding again.

"I don't know. It's really none of our business," said his father. Mr. Knight snapped open his newspaper. He had heard quite enough of Miss Carmichael.

"Hmm," mused Mrs. Knight. "I'd like to meet her properly. My curiosity is up. It's unthinkable that those young girls might have belonged to a temple."

I'd like to meet her, too, thought John. He'd especially like to meet some Indian young people. Boys would be nice, but even Indian girls would be better than getting stuck in an English boarding school.

A whistle blew. The brown grasses had given way to rich green trees and brush on the hillsides. Then the first red-tiled roofs of Ooty appeared.

Chapter 2

Reprieve From School

THE HEADMASTER of Kingsway School for Boys did not blink, but sat solid and unyielding behind the big desk.

"What do you mean, we can't enroll John because the term has already started?" The veins in Mr. Knight's face and neck were beginning to stand out. John watched his father with interest; he knew Sanford Knight was used to getting his way.

The Knights had gone directly to the school after arriving in Ooty. His father had been right—it looked very much like his old school back in Brighton, except, instead of the English Channel sparkling in the distance, the Western Ghats rose like a misty wall out of the foothills. Boys in blazers and school ties looked at him curiously and poked each other as the three Knights walked down the cool corridor. Once they had been ushered into the school office, however, it did not take them long to realize they had bumped into another type of wall: the headmaster.

"We have our rules, Mr. Knight," the balding man said patiently, his wire-rimmed glasses perched on the end of his nose. "Our winter term began in mid-January; we are now already four weeks into the term. It would be quite upsetting both for the class, and I believe for John, to try to enter at this time. My recommendation is that you wait until the summer term."

John, trying not to slouch in the uncomfortable wooden chair, held his breath. *Not have to go to school?* Was it possible that he wouldn't have to enter this English prison for a few more months? That would mean he could get acquainted with India—the India that lay out there on the plains, back in the Tinnevelly District!

"Sanford . . ." said John's mother, touching her husband's sleeve.

"Not now, Leslie," said Mr. Knight impatiently. He scowled at the headmaster, then went to stand by the window. "This is quite inconvenient, Mr. Bath. I have responsibilities; I must travel. I had hoped that John could settle into school so that my wife might join me. And I don't like him getting behind. Are you sure—?"

"Quite sure," said the headmaster. "However, since you have made the trip to Ooty, why don't we complete our interview and do the paperwork necessary to enroll John for the next term. That will be at least one thing out of the way."

And so it was done. An hour later Mr. Knight hailed a *tonga*, a two-wheeled horse carriage, and gave the name of Willingdon House to the driver. As the horse clipped along toward the inn, he stared moodily as they passed the stately Ooty Club and St. Stephen's Church.

"Sanford," Mrs. Knight tried again, "maybe it's all for the best. This gives us some more time to be together as a family, to adjust to our new surroundings. And don't forget that I have my teaching certificate; I could tutor John in most subjects."

"That's right, Father," said John. So far he had said little, hoping not to betray the wild happiness within that wanted to hoot and holler with joy. "I'll study with Mama; that way I won't get behind."

"Humph. Not exactly the same as a proper school. But I guess we'll do what we have to do."

Their bags had already been delivered by Azim to the large rambling inn, nestled among stone paths and flowering bushes. "This is lovely!" said Mrs. Knight, taking off her *topee* and walking through the airy sitting and sleeping rooms. "Let's put disappointment behind us and just enjoy our holiday!"

John felt a little guilty. He wasn't disappointed, and he was for sure going to enjoy the holiday!

The next day Leslie Knight dressed in comfortable walking clothes and shoes and set out for a hike with John; there were many walking paths from Ooty into the hills. Sanford Knight chose to go to the men's club instead to get the news.

"John, stay with your mother," he ordered. "Remain on the paths and don't go far. There are snakes and wild animals in the hills; you can't be too careful."

"Yes, Father."

The path soon left the town behind them and went up at a steep slant. The mountain forest was cool and shady under the lush cover of leaves. "Oh, lovely," murmured Mrs. Knight, stopping now and then to get her breath.

Mother and son walked in silence for half an hour, then the trees thinned and the sound of water grew louder. Rounding a bend, they were confronted with a marvelous waterfall, surrounded by outcroppings of rock overhead.

It was a few moments before John realized they weren't alone. The woman from the cog train sat on a boulder watching several of her girls splashing in the water at the foot of the falls. She was still dressed in the pale blue sari, one of the smaller children cradled in her lap.

"Why, Miss Carmichael," John heard his mother say. Mrs. Knight approached the woman and held out her hand. "I had been hoping to meet you. My name is Leslie Knight, and this is my son John. I was wondering whether the man who fell off the train had recovered."

The woman shook Mrs. Knight's hand and smiled at John. "My name is Amy Carmichael. Won't you join us? We are soaking up God's beauty, aren't we,

Blossom?" The Indian child on her lap giggled and then reached out a chubby arm.

"I think the man will be all right," the woman went on. "He has a bad concussion and is resting at the guest cottage where we are staying."

"I must admit our chance meeting yesterday has left me curious," said Mrs. Knight. "Tell me about yourself and these girls—if I'm not being too bold."

Amy Carmichael's eyes rested fondly on the girls who had tucked their skirts up and were still poking around in the water, casting curious glances in their direction. Miss Carmichael had brown eyes, surrounded by laugh wrinkles and skin tanned by the sun. John guessed she was at least forty.

"There is not much to tell," the woman said. She seemed suddenly shy. "We live just outside the village of Dohnavur in a place we call Dohnavur Fellowship. It is home to me, several godly Indian women, a few English volunteers, and many more girls like Blossom here whom God has rescued from the evil practices of the Hindu temples. A good woman here in Ooty—a Mrs. Hopewell—has made her cottage available to us so that we might have a place of retreat. Right now many of the children at Dohnavur are sick; I have brought these girls here to escape the fever.

"Now," she brightened, "tell me about yourself."

Mrs. Knight chatted briefly about their recent arrival, her husband's position as junior magistrate in Palamcottah, and their coming to Ooty to enroll John in school.

"Ah," said Miss Carmichael upon hearing that John could not enter school at mid-term. "No doubt you are deeply disappointed." She winked at John; he grinned. He liked this Amy Carmichael, whoever she was.

"You say you are a teacher, Mrs. Knight?" continued Miss Carmichael. "We have a great need for teachers at Dohnavur."

"Oh, I don't know if I could teach," John's mother said. "We are still so new to India. I have no idea what life will be like in Palamcottah, or what Sanford will expect of me as the wife of a magistrate. And, of course, I need to be tutoring John until he can start the summer term."

John wandered away from the two women toward the waterfall. The mist felt cool on his face and hair. He wondered if any of the girls playing in the water beneath the falls spoke English. "Hello," he said, standing on the bank.

The girls in the water fell silent, pressed their palms together, and bowed their heads toward him in a little *salaam*, or greeting.

John held his hands together and salaamed right back. This brought giggles from the girls, but they still kept their eyes lowered.

John wondered what to do next. How could he tell them he wanted to be friends when he could not speak their language? Then he had an idea. He sat on the bank, removed his walking shoes and socks, and stepped into the water. It was cold! He took a few more steps away from the bank; he would walk across on the stones and small boulders that dotted the mountain stream. Maybe he could show the girls how it could be done. But he was not prepared for the strength of the rushing water, and without warning a slippery rock sent him under in a big splash.

Before John knew what was happening, several small, strong hands had grasped his arms and pulled him up out of the water. Then, just as quickly, the

Indian girls had scrambled up the bank and were running toward Miss Carmichael and his mother, leaving a dripping John to make his way out of the stream.

He was embarrassed. But all his mother said when he approached the group clustered around Miss Carmichael was, "Better sit in the sun and dry off; it's quite cool in the forest."

John sat at a little distance from the group, shivering in his damp clothes and trying to regain his pride. But he could still overhear the conversation.

"You must at least come to visit us soon," Amy Carmichael was saying. "Dohnavur is only twenty miles south of Palamcottah. Bring John with you if you like! We haven't any boys—though God knows the boys of India are being trapped by the same slavery of paganism that holds the girls. Someday . . . someday God will provide. Oh. Except Arul. Arul is our first boy, a few years older than John, I believe. He is a great help and blessing, and has suffered dearly for his faith in the Lord Jesus. He could show John around. . . ."

John forgot his damp clothes. Oh! If only he could visit Dohnavur Fellowship and meet this Arul person. But . . . would his father allow it? He didn't seem too pleased about John mixing with the Indians socially, much less being friendly with Amy Carmichael, who dressed like a native, rescued little girls, and made the Hindu holy men angry.

But, then, he knew his mother was on his side. There was no way that Leslie Knight would be content to sit around sipping tea with other English ladies when an opportunity to get to know the real India—and even help its children—was being offered to her.

Chapter 3

The Money-Begging Elephant

THE HOLIDAY IN OOTY lasted two weeks. The weather in late February was sunny and moderate during the day, but downright chilly when the sun sank behind the hills. One day Mr. Knight took his wife and son to a polo match at the Ooty polo grounds. They also went riding in the hills on hired horses, dined at the Ooty Club, and poked around the Nilgiri Library. Each day's activities usually ended with tea served on the open porch of Willingdon House.

John and his mother also enjoyed several hikes into the mountain forest with Amy Carmichael and her little band. (Mr. Knight, not keen on hiking, preferred the more dignified company at the club.) As the Indian girls scampered along the trails, John thought they looked like wildflowers with brightly colored ribbons of yellow, rose, blue, and green braided into their beautiful thick black hair.

The Irish missionary and her girls left Ooty a few days before the Knights. "Forgive me if I'm being forward, but why do you travel third class?" Leslie Knight asked Miss Carmichael as they said goodbye on the Ooty train station platform.

"Because there isn't any fourth class!" Amy Carmichael laughed, and swung onto the cog train. The girls, all chattering like magpies, leaned out the windows waving goodbye until the little train disappeared.

As they turned to walk back to Willingdon House, John asked his mother, "What did she mean?"

Leslie Knight brushed away a pesky flying insect. "I'm not sure, son. She seems to think it's important to identify with the people of India, to live as they live and travel as they travel. 'All are one in Christ Jesus,' she told me. I also imagine money is limited, caring for as many children as she does. But imagine—traveling third class on those hard benches! So crowded and uncomfortable."

John silently agreed. Even traveling in first-class compartments, the trip "home" to Palamcottah was tiring. After the cog train took them down the mountain, the trip took several more days by regular train. At every station water carriers would run alongside crying, "*Hindu tunni!*" or "*Mussulman tunni!*" ("Water for Hindus and water for Muslims," Azim, their Indian servant, explained.) Food could also be purchased from vendors who prepared curries and rice dishes right on the station platform. At night, Azim let down an overhead berth on which John slept, while his parents slept on the cushioned seats below.

From the train station in Palamcottah, they were carried to the junior magistrate's house by *palanquin*—individual chairs resting on two long poles carried on the shoulders of Indians wearing only *dhotis*, loose loincloths wrapped between the legs and tucked in at the waist.

It was hotter in Palamcottah than in Ooty, but the heat was dry and bearable. The house with its walled courtyard was open and airy. Servants seemed to appear out of nowhere to unpack their bags, bring water for baths, serve four o'clock tea on the porch, and deliver *chits*—letters sent between households for communication, including several invitations from British army wives who wanted to meet Mrs. Knight.

"Do we really need this many servants, Sanford?" Mrs. Knight asked, as first one, then another appeared to do small, simple tasks.

Mr. Knight laughed. "*We* don't, but *they* do," he chuckled. "You will soon discover that the caste system in India is worse than any trade union back in England. If a servant is from the farming caste, he will weed the vegetable garden, but he won't clean the toilets—you will need to hire a sweeper to do that. On and on it goes!"

True to her word, Leslie Knight obtained a variety of schoolbooks and started John on his lessons—

three hours each morning. But they had only been back in Palamcottah for a few days when Sanford Knight, home for lunch as was his custom, announced that he had to travel on government business to Bangalore, a major city in south India about three hundred miles to the north.

"I am afraid I shall be gone for several weeks," he said to his wife. "I would like to take you with me, Leslie, but with John not in school . . . well, I simply don't have time to make the necessary arrangements to bring you both along."

"It's quite all right, Sanford," Mrs. Knight assured him. "We'll do fine. John should keep up with his lessons, and perhaps we'll have time to explore the countryside a bit."

John was disappointed at being left behind. Bangalore! He was sure a large city would be mysterious and exciting. Then he realized his father was still talking.

" . . . don't want you going about alone, Leslie. You must take one of the servants with you at all times. Azim is a good man; I will leave him here with you. One of the other servants can go with me."

Two days later Mrs. Knight and John waved goodbye as a two-wheeled *tonga* with Sanford Knight, a servant, and the luggage headed for the Palamcottah train station. But it only took a couple of days for John to grow restless. Azim fixed up an old bicycle for him to ride, but his mother felt uneasy letting him go very far on his own.

Leslie Knight was restless, too. Once lessons were

over, there was very little for an English lady to do. She went over the menus with the Indian cook, arranged the cut flowers that appeared fresh from somewhere each day, and accepted visits from bored Army wives eager to get a look at the junior magistrate's wife. But John knew his mother was uncomfortable with the endless gossip that accompanied these visits.

Then a letter arrived from Dohnavur Fellowship. "It's from Miss Carmichael, John!" Mrs. Knight exclaimed. "A note inviting us to visit Dohnavur. Why, that's the very thing. She said Dohnavur was only twenty miles from Palamcottah. We can hire a carriage or even those funny chairs on poles . . ."

"*Palanquins*, Mama." John grinned.

" . . . And your father will be gone several weeks. This would be a good time to go since I doubt he would be interested. It will be our chance to explore the Tinnevelly District, and see the villages on the way."

Mrs. Knight lost no time in sending a return message to Dohnavur that they were coming on March 10. John was hoping his mother would forget about lessons, but he saw the schoolbooks go into the bags. Azim arranged for a two-horse carriage that would take them part way; then they would have to find local transportation to take them on to Dohnavur.

They arose early, but the cook would not allow them to depart without doing justice to the large breakfast he had prepared: papaya slices, porridge, fish cakes, boiled eggs, and toast and marmalade, washed down with tea. John slid the fish cakes into his napkin when he thought no one was looking— ghastly things for breakfast, he thought.

The carriage arrived a bit later. There was a flurry of activity while the servants piled the luggage on one seat, then helped Mrs. Knight and John into the other. Azim climbed up with the hired driver.

As the horses threaded their way through the crowded dirt streets of Palamcottah and then headed south into the countryside, John had a delicious sense of freedom. The courtyard walls around their house in Palamcottah were confining; they seemed designed to keep India out. But now the road was beckoning him toward unknown adventures.

The carriage passed field after field of muddy rice paddies, where farmers were preparing the soil for planting in April and May. Some farmers guided plows behind single oxen; others used crude hand tools to break up the clods of dirt. John noticed that each paddy was surrounded by a little dirt dike. "They keep water in when the monsoons come, young sahib," Azim explained.

Most of the villages along the road were small and poor. Ragged children ran alongside the carriage crying, *"Buckshees! Buckshees!"* holding out their hands for money. Azim shouted something at them in the Tamil language and they scattered. Women crouched over fires and cooking pots outside their mud-wall and thatch-roof huts, or carried waterpots on their heads as they returned from the village well.

Noon had passed when the carriage came into a larger town called Four Lakes. John noticed a Muslim mosque with its twin minarets not far from the ornate gold dome of a Hindu temple. "The carriage must return to Palamcottah before dark," said Azim. "It is only five or six miles to Dohnavur. We can hire a bandy." Mrs. Knight and John got down from the carriage near the marketplace, and Azim paid the driver. Azim then disappeared into the market to find an ox cart for hire.

While they were waiting for Azim to return, John heard a commotion coming from the direction of the Hindu temple. A magnificent elephant decorated with richly embroidered fabric and flowing tassels came into view. Shouting and laughing, children danced about dangerously close to its enormous feet. The driver of the elephant sat on its neck and guided it toward the marketplace.

At a nearby booth, the elephant stopped and stretched its trunk into the booth. John noticed that the vendor placed something into the trunk, which the elephant swung up to its driver. Then the trunk swung back toward the vendor and rested a brief moment on the man's head.

The elephant came nearer, and suddenly the great trunk reached out toward John and Mrs. Knight. He heard his mother stifle a cry; John too felt a little frightened. What was he supposed to do? "*Buckshees! Buckshees!*" shouted some of the children. John dug in his pocket for a *four anna* Indian coin and placed it in the pink, sloppy wetness of the tip of the elephant's trunk. Back and up the great trunk swung; as it came down John thought it was going to smash into him. But instead the elephant rested its trunk gently on John's head in blessing, then lumbered on.

"Hindu elephant," said Azim's voice in John's ear. "Collects money for the temple."

The fear had passed but the excitement remained. John decided not to ask his mother whether giving money to a pagan temple was a good thing for an English Christian to do; he would never forget the feel of the elephant's trunk resting on his head.

Azim had not been able to locate an ox cart for hire, but they were hungry. The servant unpacked the lunch that the cook had sent—vegetables with rice wrapped in large green banana leaves, and fruit. They ate hungrily, sitting on their luggage, using their fingers to scoop the food into their mouths. Mrs. Knight started to giggle, then she and John nearly choked as they burst out laughing. If only Sanford Knight could see them now!

Azim finally located a bandy, which was nothing more than a covered cart pulled by two oxen. But by now the afternoon sun was beginning to slide down the western sky when they left Four Lakes and headed toward Dohnavur. The oxen were slow, barely covering three miles an hour. For a while John and his mother got out and walked alongside the cart.

As they neared the village of Dohnavur, John noticed that a young Indian girl was following them. But she seemed frightened when she saw John looking in her direction, and darted into the brush.

"Did you see that girl, Mama?"

"No. Where, dear?" said Mrs. Knight absentmind-edly. John didn't bother to reply. The girl was already gone.

In the village of Dohnavur, Azim dismounted from the cart to ask directions to the home of the Irish missionary. John thought he saw the same girl again, inching close to Azim's elbow as he talked rapidly in Tamil with an old man. John looked closely at the girl. She was maybe twelve years old and wore many gold bangles on both arms and around her ankles. But he had a hard time getting a look at her face; she looked this way and that as if afraid someone would see her, and she held a corner of her scarf over her nose and mouth.

The old man pointed west of the village, and when John looked again, the girl had disappeared.

"Just outside the village," said Azim, hopping onto the cart. Sure enough, as they left the village, they soon approached a large, walled compound. The bandy driver drove up toward an arched gate made of bricks. A small sign at the side of the gate had strange black scratchings on it, which John supposed was in the Tamil language. Underneath the scratchings were the English words, "Dohnavur Fellowship."

They had arrived.

Chapter 4

Refuge!

AZIM PULLED THE ROPE and rang the bell to announce their arrival as the bandy driver unloaded their bags. Soon the iron gates swung wide and a young Indian man greeted them with a big smile.

"Mrs. Knight! John Knight! Welcome! My name is Arul Dasan. *Amma* is expecting you."

"*Amma*?" John whispered quizzically to Azim.

"*Amma* means 'mother' in Tamil," said the servant.

Arul looked about eighteen or nineteen years old, John thought, as they followed the young man into the compound toward a one-story house with a wide porch. Amy Carmichael was sitting on the floor of the porch with several Indian women feeding a one-year-old baby with her fingers. When the little party came close, Miss Carmichael jumped up to greet them.

"Leslie! John! I am so delighted that you have come! And this is . . . ?"

"Azim, our . . . er, servant," said Mrs. Knight.

"We are all servants here!" smiled Miss Carmichael, shifting the baby to her hip and giving Leslie Knight a hug to take away the awkwardness of the moment. "Come and join us for our meal."

She introduced the other women workers. "These are our *accals*, big sisters to the children." The *accals* beamed big smiles and greeted them with their palms pressed together in gentle salaams.

John and Arul sat with their plates of food on the steps to the porch a little way from the women. Azim accepted the food but walked away from the house to eat. John looked around at the other small houses scattered about the compound. All the buildings were turning a deep blue as the sky reddened in the west. Some had wavy red-tile roofs, others had straw thatch, though they looked more sturdy than the ones he'd seen in the villages along the way. He wondered where the girls were . . . then the sound of children singing came floating through the twilight.

Arul nodded toward the music. "The little ones are singing praise to God!"

John swallowed the last of his rice. "Arul," he said, "how did you come here? I mean, there are no boys . . . just girls."

Arul grinned. "I heard the Word of God and

wanted to follow Jesus. But my family was very upset. They beat me and threatened to rub pepper in my eyes. So, I came to my new home with Amma."

"How old were you?"

"Ten or eleven. I forget." The grin flashed again. "This is my new family. I work hard to help Amma; she lets me stay."

John sat staring out into the deepening twilight. Birds twittered their good nights from the tamarind trees. It felt strange to hear someone talk about being beaten just because he wanted to be a Christian. In England, everyone John knew was a Christian . . . well, at least they went to church on Sunday. It was the expected thing to do, like honoring your parents and the British flag. John believed in God, and of course he knew that Jesus was God's Son . . . but what did it mean to "follow Jesus" in the way Arul was talking about? Would he be willing to call himself a Christian if his family threatened to rub pepper in his eyes?

A bell rang.

"Someone's at the gate," said Arul, getting up. "We aren't expecting anyone. I wonder who . . . ?" He walked quickly toward the outer gate. John followed him at a trot.

The bell rang insistently, and as Arul and John got closer, they could hear the faint sound of fists beating on the gate and urgent cries. Throwing back the bar, Arul pulled on the gate and it swung in. A frightened young girl took a step backward, as if afraid of being struck. Then she threw herself at the boys' feet crying a single word over and over.

John stared, his mouth open. It was the girl who had been following them on the road to Dohnavur!

"What is she saying? What does she want?" John asked anxiously as Arul bent down and lifted the girl to her feet.

"Refuge! She wants refuge," the older boy said. "Quick—shut the gate!"

John hastily barred the gate again, then caught up with Arul and the weeping girl as they made their way toward the main house where Amy Carmichael and John's mother were sitting with the Indian women. As the group on the porch heard the commotion, Miss Carmichael handed the baby to one of the Indian *accals* and came rushing down the steps.

"Dear child!" she said, drawing the girl into a warm embrace in the folds of her sari.

"There, there, you are safe here." The "mother" of Dohnavur Fellowship brought the unexpected visitor onto the porch and sat down, holding the girl, big as she was, on her lap. The girl's dark arms went around Miss Carmichael's neck and clung to her tightly.

Arul tapped John on the shoulder. "Come. We will say good-night. Let us leave them."

John looked at his mother, who was similarly being drawn away by the Indian women. She nodded at him and gave him a little smile as if to say, "I'm sure it's all right. Go with Arul." So he followed the older boy through the compound, which was dark now, except for the light of the moon.

Arul took him to a small thatch-roofed cottage with a little porch made of cane. Inside Arul lit a lantern. It had only one room, which was quite bare except for a writing table, a chair, a cupboard in one corner and three wooden bed frames. Woven rope within the frame served as the sleeping surface.

"*Charpoy*," Arul said, pointing at the wooden frames. "Beds. For you, me, and Azim."

Arul disappeared for a few moments and came back with John's bag. "Azim says he will sleep outside." Arul shrugged.

The *charpoy* looked rather uncomfortable, even with a blanket covering the woven rope. But it had been a long, exciting day, and within moments John was sound asleep.

✧ ✧ ✧ ✧

John awoke to the sound of birds in the tamarind trees. At first he didn't know where he was, but then the events of the previous day came flooding back. He was at Dohnavur Fellowship, sharing a small cottage of sun-baked bricks with an Indian boy.

John sat up. The room was empty. He dressed quickly and stepped out into the bright sunshine. Azim was waiting for him on the little porch.

"Young *sahib*, your mother waits for you at the main house," said the servant.

John heard childish laughter. He saw several Indian women and older girls taking several babies for a walk along one of the paths, either pushing buggies in which two or three babies sat or holding older tots by the hand.

Leslie Knight and Amy Carmichael were talking on the porch as John and Azim approached. "Ah, there you are, John," said Miss Carmichael. "I was just discussing our young visitor last night, and my idea affects you as well. Please, help yourself to a little breakfast and join us."

A plate of sliced fruit, some muffin-like cakes, and a pot of tea were laid out on a little table, along with plates and cups. John helped himself, then sat on the floor near his mother.

"I was just telling your mother that it is obvious this young girl is from a very high caste, and it may be difficult for her to mix with the other girls here at first. I don't know her story—she was too exhausted last night to tell me. But . . . why, here she is!"

John had heard no one, but there, standing in the

doorway was the girl, a shy smile on her face. Miss Carmichael held out her arms, and the girl went straight to her. She shook her head no when offered some food, but stood leaning against Amy Carmichael.

"Come, child," said Miss Carmichael, "we must know more about you." She took the girl's hands in her own and said something in Tamil. The girl then spoke rapidly, the smile disappearing and her eyes once again looking like a frightened rabbit. She pointed several times to the south and once she pointed to John and his mother.

While the white woman and the nut-brown girl talked, John studied the girl. Her face was heart-shaped, framed by jet-black hair pulled back into a braid. She wore jeweled earrings and a gold necklace. Her sari, a delicate rose color, was edged with gold and green. Her feet were bare, but as he had noticed before, she wore gold bangles on her ankles, as well as both arms. She was the most beautiful girl he had ever seen.

Finally Amy Carmichael spoke in English, almost to herself. "We shall call you Jewel, for God has plucked you out of the dirt into His kingdom of light, and longs to polish your heart to shine for Him."

Then she turned to Mrs. Knight and John. "Jewel comes from the merchant caste; her father, a widower, was quite a wealthy man. But he died last year, leaving Jewel in the care of her uncle. In his will, the father named Jewel as his heir, to be inherited when she becomes eighteen, or when she marries, whichever comes first. Her uncle wants to get hold of her money, so he has arranged for her to be married to a distant relative of his—an old man of fifty!"

"Oh, no!" cried Mrs. Knight. "Why, she can't be more than twelve years old!"

Amy Carmichael shook her head sadly. "Oh, if only it were forbidden! But child-brides are quite common in India—young girls of twelve and thirteen, married and having children before they are even out of their teens. If the husband is old and dies, a girl becomes a widow who is blamed for her husband's death and abused as a household slave for the rest of her life by his relatives."

"She followed us—from Four Lakes, I think," John said. "I saw her twice before we arrived last night."

Miss Carmichael smiled. "You did not know you were leading her to us, but all things work together in God's plan. She is from Vallioor—that is the town where the post office and telegraph are located. She had only heard of the white *Amma* and the big home 'where children grow up good.' She ran away as far as Four Lakes when she saw white people traveling by bandy and decided to follow, hoping that you would lead her here."

Just then Arul came running up to the house. "Amma! There is a man at the gate—very angry! He has come for the girl!" Then he spoke rapidly in Tamil.

The effect on the girl was electric. She immediately cried out and threw herself at Amy's feet. Miss

Carmichael lifted her up and hushed her in Tamil. John could now hear the bell ringing furiously at the gate.

"Arul, let the man in," said Miss Carmichael calmly. She drew the girl down upon the bench she was sitting on and placed a protective arm around her. Some of the Indian women workers and girls, hearing the commotion, gathered at a distance to watch.

In a few minutes Arul came back with an Indian man who strode angrily up to the house. He was wearing a *topi*, a cloth hat with no brim, a long tunic and tight leggings, and carried a stick. Azim seemed to appear from no-where and stood in the man's way; Arul also turned around on the steps and faced the adversary. The little group on the porch—Amy Carmichael, Jewel, Mrs. Knight, and John—stood up and faced the man, though Jewel hid her face in Amy's arm.

The man's eyes were narrowed and his face hard. He spoke rapidly in Tamil and pointed at Jewel.

"What is he saying, Arul?" John whispered, standing slightly behind the older boy.

"He says she is his niece, his legal ward, and she must come home with him at once."

Miss Carmichael said nothing at first, but gently turned Jewel and encouraged her to lift her face and look at her uncle. Then she spoke to the man in Tamil. Arul quietly interpreted for John.

"Amma asks if the child is to be married; the uncle says yes, it is all arranged. . . . Now Amma is asking Jewel if she wants to be married." John saw Jewel shake her head and she spoke a single word forcefully; even without knowing Tamil, John knew it was no. "Now Amma is asking Jewel if she wants to go with her uncle. . . . Jewel says no, she wants to stay here. . . . The uncle says, 'So? She is only a girl; it is not for her to decide.' . . . But Amma says it is her choice; she will stay here."

This made the uncle furious. He shook the stick first at Jewel, then at Amy Carmichael, and let loose a torrent of angry words. Azim took a step forward, and the man backed off. With a few more words and threatening gestures, he turned on his heel and strode back toward the gate.

"What did he say?" breathed Mrs. Knight, whose

face had suddenly turned quite white.

"He said we are guilty of kidnapping, and we haven't heard the last from him yet," said Miss Carmichael. "Arul, be sure the gate is locked. We will need to take extra precautions for a while." As Arul ran off, Amy walked over to the little cluster of girls who were watching, gave a few reassuring hugs, then sent them off to their tasks.

Amy Carmichael returned to the porch and said, "Leslie, I believe God has sent you and John for this very time. Let me tell you my idea. . . ."

Chapter 5

Good Friday Comes on Easter

Amy Carmichael's idea was simple: she wanted Mrs. Knight and John to stay several weeks to help care for Jewel. "The *accals* and I have our hands full with the other children—we have over thirty right now, and many are babies! Jewel will need special care because of her caste. Until God breaks down the barriers, we should respect her caste restrictions as much as possible. But she will be lonely not mixing with the other girls and will need a companion. And, given the danger, it would be helpful to have Azim and John around the compound to assist Arul."

"But we don't even speak her language!" protested Mrs. Knight.

Amy smiled. "Arul can interpret when needed.

But love is the same in any language."

Mrs. Knight had a good many objections. They had only planned to visit a week. What if her husband came home while they were away? What about John's schooling? Was she neglecting her duties at Palamcottah?

"Those are reasonable concerns, Leslie," said Amy Carmichael. "Seek God's will. He will show you what to do. But I believe that your arrival on the same day Jewel found us is not a mere coincidence."

Later Mrs. Knight and John went walking by the stream that ran alongside the west wall of the Dohnavur compound. "I hardly know what to think," confessed his mother.

John shrugged. "You can tutor me here as well as at home, Mama."

"Well . . . I suppose that's true."

"And what would you be doing in Palamcottah? Sipping tea with the colonel's wife and having all those servants hovering around doing everything except your thinking!"

Mrs. Knight laughed. "When you put it *that* way . . ." Then she sighed. "But I would hate to be gone when your father returns. That seems unfair."

John picked up a stone and sent it skipping into the stream. "Send Father a message. Just ask him to let us know when he's coming home. We can at least stay *until* then."

"I guess you're right." Mrs. Knight was silent for a few minutes. "I've never really thought of seeking God's will when trying to make a decision. I mean, we keep the commandments and go to church faithfully, but—"

"Why, you are a good Christian, Mama!"

"Hmm. Maybe. But Amy Carmichael lives as if Jesus Christ were right here in India, and she were one of His disciples."

That afternoon Mrs. Knight told Amy they would stay until her husband returned from his business trip. Miss Carmichael immediately held a little prayer meeting to praise God. Azim was sent to Vallioor to telegraph a message to the household at Palamcottah and another to Sanford Knight in Bangalore. Jewel moved in with Mrs. Knight in the Guest House.

The days settled into a routine: Mrs. Knight tutored John in the mornings while the Dohnavur girls were busy in their schoolrooms. Jewel sat near Mrs. Knight weaving on a hand loom. Sometimes Arul sat in on the lessons between chores. At these times, the Guest House schoolroom often degenerated into a language swap.

"How do you say 'I'm hungry'? . . . 'Good morning'? . . . 'Go away'?" John would pester Arul. The English boy's efforts to say things in Tamil often triggered a giggle from Jewel. But the language swap intrigued the girl; she crept closer, and soon began to try out a few English words.

In the afternoons, John helped Arul with the maintenance work on the Dohnavur grounds. *Amma*— as everyone seemed to call Amy Carmichael—wanted a new garden to help feed the growing Dohnavur family, so Arul and John spent days digging up a new plot and hauling stones away. The older girls could often be seen in the other gardens weeding around the new green shoots and hauling water from the wells to keep the ground moist. At other times John would see them heading for the Weaving Shed or the Milk Kitchen.

In the evenings, the Dohnavur "family" gathered in the House of Prayer for worship and prayer, led by Amy or one of the older Indian women. John patrolled the compound with Azim or Arul, making sure the gates were secure. He loved to hear the girls sing; their clear voices seemed to rise in the hot, still air and hang like a canopy among the leaves of the tall palm trees.

Several weeks passed; March melted into April. On the Saturday before Easter Arul handed John a bucket with a murky brown mixture in it. "The babies are gone today; the *accals* have taken them on an outing. We need to put new floors in the nurseries."

New floors? Whatever did Arul mean? John followed the older boy to one of the thatch-roofed cottages that housed the babies. The simple furniture and sleeping mats had been hauled outside. Arul showed John how to slop the wet mash onto the floor and spread it evenly with a brush.

"What is this stuff?" John asked. It felt like warm mud.

"Cow dung."

"*Cow dung!*" John dropped the brush and leaped

to his feet. His stomach turned as he thought of his hands in the sloppy mess. "I won't do it," he muttered and stalked to the doorway. This was too much, he thought. It was one thing to dig a garden and haul stones for Dohnavur Fellowship, but he drew the line at sticking his hands in a mess of manure. He was a guest, a volunteer, for heaven's sake!

A woman's gentle voice at his side startled him. "May I have that bucket?" Amy Carmichael said. She picked up the bucket he had abandoned and joined Arul on hands and knees, spreading the thick liquid on the floor. John reddened and watched awkwardly from the door.

When the floor was covered, Amy straightened her back and stepped outside. "At Dohnavur Fellowship, John, all work, great and small, clean or dirty, is done for God." She smiled, handed him the bucket, and disappeared around the corner of the cottage.

John sighed.

"But . . . why cow dung?" he finally asked Arul.

"The cow is a useful animal." Arul grinned. "Dry cow dung makes good fuel. And when it's dried, dung has no smell. On the other hand, fresh dung is mixed with water and spread on the floor. When it dries, it makes a soft floor—much more friendly than hard English floors! Soft to the feet, warm in the cool season."

John picked up the brush and bucket and followed Arul to the next nursery. He'd try not to think about it.

When both baby nurseries had new "floors," the two boys washed up at one of the wells, then walked toward the main house. As they approached, they saw a two-horse carriage and driver standing inside the compound. A tall white man wearing a sun helmet stood talking with John's mother on the steps of the porch.

"Father!" yelled John, dropping the bucket and running the last few yards.

Sanford Knight smiled and gave his son a manly handshake and a clap on the shoulder. "I see you've been busy, John."

John blushed. "I . . . I need to change my clothes. Been doing a little dirty work."

"I can see that," said his father. "Get changed; I'd like you to join your mother and me for a talk . . . at the Guest House, did you say, Leslie?"

John quickly changed his clothes in Arul's cottage, then found his parents. "Didn't you get the message about my arrival home, Leslie?" his father was saying.

"I'm afraid not, Sanford, or I would surely have been back in Palamcottah. Someone here has to pick up the mail in Valioor. Your message is probably sitting there now. I'm terribly sorry you had to come all this way for us."

"What is this about helping to care for a runaway girl—Jewel, is that her name? Really, Leslie! You know how I feel about interfering in the domestic affairs of the Indian people."

"I know, Sanford. But it's different when a child runs to your arms because she is terrified of being married to a man five times her age."

Sanford Knight frowned. "Miss Carmichael means well, Leslie, but there are legal consequences to her actions. I don't want my own wife and son *breaking the law*. After all, I am junior magistrate for the Tinnevelly District!"

John sat on the steps of the porch while his parents talked. Maybe his father was right on this . . . he hadn't thought that they could be breaking the law. He wondered what would happen to Jewel when they left. He knew already that he would miss Dohnavur Fellowship.

Azim, on the other hand, was visibly relieved that they were going home. Things were too mixed up at this place, in his opinion. White women and boys did servants' work; servants were invited to sit and eat; caste distinctions were being lost, he complained frequently to Arul.

Sanford Knight agreed to wait until after the Easter celebration the following morning to begin the journey home with his family. Just before dawn the three Knights, with Jewel clinging sadly to Leslie, joined the crowd of excited girls and their *accals* in front of the main house.

"He is risen!" people greeted one another in English and Tamil.

"He is risen indeed! Alleluia!" came the response.

The crowd made their way along the paths, around the school and girls' cottages, through the round brick gateways that marked each section of the compound, to God's Garden.

"Why do they call it that?" John asked Arul.

"Babies are buried here who became sick and died. But there are no markers; just flowers and trees. The babies are in heaven—God's Garden."

In the garden Amy led them in singing Easter hymns in both English and Tamil. The sun rose red and glorious, bathing the sky in pink, shimmering light. The birds set off a joyful racket. *Was it something like this on the day Jesus broke out of His tomb?* John wondered.

The group finally wandered back toward the main

house for an Easter breakfast picnic. Jewel shook her head no when offered something to eat; she would prepare something later. As they sat on the ground enjoying the fresh fruit and breads made especially for the occasion, the front gate bell began ringing. Arul trotted off to answer it.

"Probably the carriage," said John's father. "I told the driver to be here early."

But it was not the carriage. Two men walked resolutely into the compound behind Arul. One of them was Jewel's uncle; the other, an Indian policeman.

Amy Carmichael rose to meet them. Leslie Knight drew a protective arm around Jewel, who was shivering with fright.

Jewel's uncle waved a paper at Amy and sneered a few brief words in Tamil. John heard Arul suck in his breath. "Police orders," Arul said quietly to the Knights. "Jewel must return with her uncle."

Amy was about to say something when Sanford Knight got to his

By Order
of the
District Police

feet and approached her.

"Miss Carmichael," he said. "I realize I am a guest here. But I am also a court official of the Tinnevelly District. And I must tell you that you have no legal right to keep this girl, no matter how tragic you think her situation. The penalty for ignoring a police order could be prison."

"I don't care for myself," Amy said quietly.

"But you must think of all the persons in your care. If you wish, you could file a counter suit in court and let a judge decide what should happen."

All voices fell silent. Only the birds in the tamarind trees continued their racket. Then, slowly, the "mother" of Dohnavur walked over to Jewel and bent down. She spoke first in Tamil, then in English. "Jewel, the paper says you must go with your uncle. But we will fight. I will go to court and ask if you can come here to Dohnavur to live—permanently. In the meantime, Jesus your Friend will be with you."

The uncle, realizing no one would stop him, strode over to Jewel and pulled her roughly by the arm.

Suddenly Jewel began to scream and kick. The Indian policeman took her other arm, and the two men half carried, half pushed the girl toward the gate. John heard Amy gasp, "Have mercy, Lord!" and his mother broke into sobs. John took an involuntary step, but his father laid a restraining hand on his shoulder. He watched helplessly as the trio disappeared through the gate. But Jewel's loud wails could be heard for a long time.

John jerked away from his father's hand and walked quickly away from the picnic area. Hot tears stung his eyes. Easter? Resurrection? It felt more like a crucifixion.

Chapter 6

Swami-Lover

THE TRIP HOME to Palamcottah was tense. John knew his father was probably right—legally. But it seemed so *wrong* to just stand there and let that evil man drag Jewel away against her will.

His mother cried off and on all the way home. "There, there, my dear," Sanford Knight tried to comfort her. "You can't possibly rescue all the girls whose relatives arrange a child-marriage. Admittedly, it's a bad custom, but it is legal."

"Then change the law!" snapped his wife. She blew her nose on his handkerchief. "I'm sorry, Sanford. I know it's not your fault; you're just the magistrate. But even one child forced into that kind of legal slavery is . . . is a *sin!*"

The month of May was the dry hot season at its

worst, with temperatures soaring over one hundred degrees. Mr. Knight wanted to send his wife and John up to Ooty to escape the heat, but she declined, saying the family had been apart too much already. John was going to start school in June; they would travel to Ooty then.

The monsoon rains came right on time in June, bringing joyous dancing in the streets as the rice paddies filled with water and the parched earth received its yearly drink. But it made for miserable traveling by train as the Knights headed for the Kingsway School for Boys in Ooty. The train compartments had to be closed up and the humid heat was stifling, even in first class. But as they switched to the cog train for the last climb up the Nilgiri Hills, John leaned out the train window, letting the cooler moist air bathe his face.

The cog train was packed with boys returning to school and their families. John looked around, wondering if he'd be able to make a friend. He had been lonely in Palamcottah and missed Arul's friendship, even if the Indian boy was several years older. John sighed. Well, it was school now and he'd have to make the best of it.

He was assigned a room in the dormitory with two other boys from his class. After Azim deposited John's luggage, Mr. Knight steered John's mother away quickly. "He'll get on better if we don't wait around," he murmured to her.

The boys seemed friendly enough as they shook hands and picked bunks. "You're the new boy, eh?"

said one, a tall lanky fellow. "I'm Jim; this is Torry. Irish, he is!" Jim gave the red-headed Torry a friendly poke in the ribs.

"Isn't Ooty a hoot?" said Torry. "'Course it's school, but it beats sitting out the monsoons down in the towns. What a steam bath!"

"Beats rubbing elbows with all the swamis, too," snorted Jim.

John was puzzled. "Swamis? You mean *swami*, the Hindu holy men?"

Jim laughed. "Swamis, wamis, it doesn't matter. All the native boys and their ugly gods. They give me the creeps. Never know what they're thinking."

John was silent, unsure how to respond. Finally he said, "Not all Indians are Hindu or Muslim; some are Christian."

"Or pretending to be," said Jim, "just to get on with the British."

"No, really," said John. "I have a friend—his name is Arul Dasan. He became a Christian and his family threatened to rub pepper in his eyes."

"There, you see?" Torry said. "Totally barbaric. These people are not at all civilized."

John shut his mouth into a thin line. The conversation was going in a direction he didn't like. He busied himself lining up his books on the little shelf above his study desk.

"Hey, what about this Arul fellow?" Jim persisted. "He is actually your friend? How did you meet him?"

"At Dohnavur Fellowship," John said reluctantly, stuffing his suitcases under the bed. "My mother and I stayed there a month, helping to take care of a girl who was going to be married as a child-bride." The moment it was out of his mouth, however, John was sorry he said anything.

"Ooooh. A *girl*," Torry hooted.

"Not just a girl—a *native* girl," said Jim, rolling his eyes. The two boys flopped on their beds, laughing.

John straightened up and marched to the door. He had to get out before he said something he would regret.

"Hey, don't go away mad, old man," Jim laughed. "It's just that we've never had a *swami-lover* for a roommate before." And the two boys punched each other's arms gleefully as John escaped into the hallway.

Miserably, John loosened his Kingsway tie and pushed his hands into the pockets of his blazer as he made his way down the stairway to the first floor. He walked over to the school office and asked to see the headmaster. After a fifteen-minute wait, John was ushered into the office.

"Hmm, young Knight is it?" said Mr. Bath, the headmaster.

"Yes, sir."

"Settling in all right?"

"Yes, sir. I guess. But what does Kingsway offer in languages?"

"Why, all the classical languages, of course: Latin, Greek; and French, German—"

"Any Indian languages? Tamil, for instance?"

The headmaster just looked at John. "Indian languages? Why, no, it's hardly necessary. Most high-ranking Indians in British India speak English."

"But not the people, sir. I realize that India has many languages and dialects, but Tamil is the most common language of this area of south India where my father is commissioned as magistrate. I am interested in learning Tamil."

The headmaster pursed his lips and tapped a pencil on his desk. "Interesting . . . interesting. Well, I'm afraid we can't help you, Mr. Knight. We have no Indian teachers at Kingsway. British for the British, Indian for the Indian, you know. But, hmmm . . ." Mr. Bath got up from the big desk and looked out the window over the town of Ooty nestled in the folds of the Nilgiri Hills. "There is a young Indian lawyer who speaks both English and Tamil who lives here in Ooty. He might be able to tutor you. Here . . ."

The headmaster scribbled a name on a slip of paper and handed it across the desk. Then he shook his finger at John. "But I warn you, Mr. Knight, learning Tamil is a hobby, to be done in your spare time, which is rare at Kingsway. If I hear that you are neglecting your regular studies, you will be ordered to stop, do you understand?"

John nodded and backed out the door with the slip of paper. He looked at the name: "Mr. Rabur, Woodcock Lodge." Pocketing the paper, John made a vow: he would certainly not mention language lessons to Torry and Jim.

❖ ❖ ❖ ❖

John was kept busy with his lessons at Kingsway and only got to see his mother and father, who stayed on at Willingdon House for a one-week holiday, on the following Sunday afternoon. But after having supper at the Ooty Club with his parents, John refused a *tonga* ride back to the school and said he'd like to walk.

Woodcock Lodge was not far from the club, a charming rooming house for single men doing business in Ooty. Mr. Rabur was a little surprised to be paid a visit from an English schoolboy, but seemed pleased at John's request for tutoring in Tamil.

"Most unusual, young *sahib*," chuckled the young Indian lawyer. "I am honored. What do you say—

Sunday afternoons? It is not enough; Tamil is a difficult language. You will have to study during the week as well."

"Yes, sir," grinned John. "I will work hard."

❖ ❖ ❖ ❖

John managed to get along reasonably well with Jim and Torry, in spite of their constant teasing. "Hey, swami-lover, we need a goalie for soccer"; "Ah-ha, swami-lover has a letter! Must be from his native girl!"

The letter in question was from his mother, dated July 2, 1909. "My dear son . . ." it began.

The rains keep us indoors much of the time. I imagine it is the same for you. (Better for studying!) But unfortunately the soccer field will be soggy. Never mind the mud; play hard!

I heard from Miss Carmichael. She has petitioned for a court hearing this month to receive custody of Jewel until a trial date can be set to resolve her situation. Your father feels she has embarked on a hopeless task. And it may be so; she desperately needs a sympathetic lawyer. . . .

Lawyer! John could not get his mother's letter out of his mind the next time he went to Woodcock Lodge for his Tamil lesson. Even though he had only known Mr. Rabur a few weeks, he found himself telling the young Indian lawyer the whole story of meeting Miss Carmichael, the trip to Dohnavur, and Jewel pounding on the gate crying, "Refuge! Refuge!" and her uncle dragging her away on Easter.

Mr. Rabur listened quietly. When John was finished he said, "Hmm. An interesting case."

John grew bold. "Could you help Miss Carmichael, Mr. Rabur? I don't know how I could pay your fee, but . . ."

The Indian lawyer stood at the window of his

sitting room and watched the clouds wrapping the hills in a thick fog. "I have to go to Palamcottah next week. I may inquire into the case; I'll see what I can do. But, young *sahib*, I promise nothing."

John grinned. He fairly flew off the porch of Woodcock Lodge when the lesson was over . . . and nearly crashed headlong into Jim and Torry, who were standing on the stone-lined path outside.

"So, what's this?" hooted Jim. "Our friend mysteriously disappears every Sunday afternoon—and here he is, visiting a rooming house of the local variety."

"A girl, Mr. Knight? Are you dating?" teased Torry.

"Very funny," said John. He started walking rapidly back toward the school. He didn't want to explain to these two rascals about Mr. Rabur and Tamil lessons. But the two boys badgered him all the way back to Kingsway, so finally John said, "My father's a magistrate, right? So I got a letter from my mother about some legal business; she asked me to deliver a message to a lawyer here in Ooty. Now, is that all right with you?"

It wasn't exactly the truth, but close enough, he thought.

"Oooh, touchy, touchy. Why didn't you say so in the first place?" said Jim. He messed up John's hair and ran off laughing with Torry. John sighed. Jim and Torry were all right some of the time, but he wished he had some real friends.

Mr. Rabur was gone to Palamcottah the next

Sunday, so John had to wait two weeks before he heard if anything happened. Borrowing a schoolmate's bicycle, he splashed through the Ooty streets to Woodcock Lodge in a downpour. He was getting tired of the monsoons—even if it was "just like home" in rainy England.

"Come in, young *sahib!*" smiled Mr. Rabur. "You will need to dry yourself by the fire."

John accepted a cup of hot tea and stretched his wet feet toward the fire in Mr. Rabur's sitting room. Then he said: "Did you meet with success in Palamcottah?"—in perfect Tamil.

Mr. Rabur threw back his head and laughed. "You have been working! I am proud of you. And yes, I have news."

The young Indian lawyer had gone to the magistrate's office in Palamcottah and arranged to meet Miss Carmichael before the hearing. Mr. Rabur offered his services free of charge—a favor "for a friend," he said. "At the hearing—"

"Did my father hear the case?" John interrupted. "He's the junior magistrate in Palamcottah."

"No . . . this was an older gentleman, due to retire this year," said Mr. Rabur.

"The senior magistrate," said John. "Well, go on."

At the hearing, both lawyers presented their clients' petitions. The other lawyer said his client was the legal guardian of his niece, and the marriage was all arranged. Mr. Rabur said the child was violently opposed to the marriage and had run away once. She wanted to live at Dohnavur Fellowship and go to school. His client, Miss Carmichael, was petitioning the court for temporary custody until the matter could be decided by the court. Mr. Rabur argued that the child's interests should be taken into account and the custody allowed to give time for a proper case to be prepared—by both sides. If the child remained with her uncle, what was to prevent the marriage from taking place before the case could be decided?

"I am most happy to report that the magistrate ruled in favor of Miss Carmichael—for now," said Mr. Rabur.

"That's it?" said John. "Just like that? Jewel went home with Miss Carmichael? Wahoo!" he shouted.

"It's not quite that simple," cautioned Mr. Rabur. "Because the matter has still not been decided, the magistrate respected the relatives' wishes that Jewel be required to 'keep caste'—that is, she may not eat food prepared by others outside her caste or eat with others not of her own caste; and further, she may not change her religion. This was spelled out in a *yadast*, or agreement between the parties."

John frowned. "That means she will have to cook and eat alone; she is the only one of her caste at Dohnavur. And—pardon me, Mr. Rabur—but it is hard to be at Dohnavur Fellowship and not desire to be a Christian."

"No pardons needed, young *sahib*," Mr. Rabur smiled. "I, too, am a follower of Jesus. It is for that reason I have agreed to help Miss Carmichael prepare for the upcoming trial."

Chapter 7

Fire!

SCHOOL WAS OUT by mid-October for "winter break" and John managed the train trip from Ooty to Palamcottah by himself. The "cool season" had eased the temperatures to seventy or eighty degrees on the plains, and the fully ripened rice fields beside the train tracks waved gently in the path of the harvesters.

After four months in very British Ooty, John had almost forgotten the crowds in the Indian towns. As he waited in line at the station to get his ticket, four or five people crushed behind him, waving *rupees* over his shoulder trying to get their own tickets.

He had done well in school—a report which pleased Sanford Knight. John answered questions about classes, sports, teachers, and other students over lunch on the porch of the big house in

Palamcottah. He decided to say nothing about being heckled by the other boys.

John was glad to see his mother looking well and rested. "It's the cool season," she smiled. "This is India at its best!"

After his father had returned to court, John asked, "What is happening at Dohnavur? When is the trial? Have you seen Jewel or Arul or Miss Carmichael?"

His mother laughed. "One question at a time! No, the trial date keeps getting delayed. The uncle's lawyer keeps filing this motion or that complaint—I don't understand all the legal issues. And yes, I have been going to Dohnavur about once a month to volunteer for five or six days. Jewel is blossoming, although she complains about having to cook and eat alone. Amma tells Jewel it is her 'cross to bear' for Jesus right now. And Arul always asks about you."

"He does?" John was pleased. "Can we . . . is it all right if I go along the next time you go to Dohnavur?"

John's mother nodded. "I think so. Your father says I am too involved in Amy Carmichael's work, of which he doesn't fully approve. And I must say, he is not alone. I have heard both British and Indians criticize her. But he agreed to the once-a-month visits as long as they don't conflict with the social obligations that come along with being the magistrate's wife."

A few days after John's arrival back home, a letter arrived from Dohnavur Fellowship.

"Several of the *accals* and many of the children are sick," Leslie Knight said, reading the letter quickly. "And Jewel's uncle tried to snatch her when she went to the market in Four Lakes with the other girls. Fortunately, she eluded him and got back safely. But Amy Carmichael wants to know if we—you and I, John—could come and help them for a few days."

Mr. Knight reluctantly agreed, providing Azim went with them. And so once more John found himself on the way to Dohnavur. He remembered that first trip into the countryside six months ago—and the temple elephant that "blessed" him with its trunk!

At Four Lakes, they once again let the rented carriage return to Palamcottah and took a *bandy* the last few miles. As the covered ox cart drew near to the arched brick gate of Dohnavur Fellowship, John thought he saw two figures slink into the trees and underbrush. But the late afternoon sun shone in his eyes and he couldn't be sure.

Arul was delighted to see his young friend and laughed aloud when John said, "I am glad to see you again," in Tamil.

Azim looked startled when John spoke Tamil. John

had given away his little secret; he had enjoyed picking up a few things that Azim said in Tamil when the servant thought he didn't understand.

Jewel came running to meet them, all smiles. When she saw John, she stopped and shyly pressed her hands together in a *salaam*. Then her smile broadened. "*Annachie!*" she said.

"*Annachie?*" John asked, turning to Arul. He had not learned that word in Tamil. "What does she mean?"

Arul grinned. "*Annachie* means 'elder brother.' You and me—that is the name Jewel calls us: *annachie*."

A strange warm feeling gripped John, and for a moment he couldn't speak. Brother. Yes, that is how he felt about Arul: an older brother. And Jewel seemed like a younger sister.

"How do you say 'younger sister' in Tamil?" he finally asked Arul.

"*Tungachie.*"

"*Tungachie.*" John rolled the word on his tongue. Then he pointed from himself to Jewel, pressed his palms together in a *salaam*, and said, "Jewel, *tungachie.*"

Jewel clapped a hand over her mouth, suppressing a giggle. Then she flew on bare feet back to the group of older girls playing with several babies under a large tamarind tree. That was when John noticed that the bangles were gone and Jewel's arms and ankles were bare.

"What happened to all of Jewel's jewels?" he asked

his mother as they made their way to the main house to see Amy Carmichael.

Azim muttered something under his breath in Tamil about a woman's jewels showing her family's status and attracting a suitable husband. John pretended he hadn't heard.

"I'm not sure," said Mrs. Knight. "The last time I was here, the bangles were gone. I think she became aware that the Indian women here have laid aside their jewels to show that they love Jesus more than wealth. And one day Jewel just took them off."

Amy Carmichael smiled and welcomed them warmly, but her eyes were tired and her face pale. That was when John and his mother realized Amy herself was sick. Leslie Knight stayed with Amy while John went to unpack in Arul's little cottage. As before, Azim refused a bed inside.

Then Arul showed John around the compound. The garden they had dug last March had produced many vegetables to help feed the Dohnavur family. In God's Garden, little bouquets of flowers decorated a new mound of fresh dirt.

"One of the babies died last week," Arul said quietly. "A temple child. It often happens. A child is snatched from living death, but Satan attacks with sickness. But death has no power here. We go to live with Jesus."

As they passed the baby nurseries, Arul teased, "You are just in time to help spread new floors!"

John gagged and made a face. Arul laughed.

"Don't worry. We did it last week. But . . ." The older boy pointed to the thatch roofs. "Amma wants to rebuild the nurseries. Termites are eating the walls, and—"

"Didn't I hear the children singing a little song about termites 'trying to be good' by working hard?" John laughed. "But my Tamil is not very good yet!"

Arul laughed, too. "Yes, yes, you are right! Amma wrote the termite song for the little children!" Then Arul's smile faded. "But we are worried. Jewel's uncle makes many threats to burn these houses. Thatch roofs are very dangerous. Every night we must watch."

As it turned out, John, Arul, and Azim patrolled the wall surrounding the Fellowship each night and slept during the day. Mrs. Knight insisted that Amy Carmichael go to bed while she nursed the Indian *accals* who were sick. A temporary clinic was set up in the main house for the babies and children who were sick. The older girls moved into the nurseries to help take care of the healthy babies.

Several days passed, and no more children became sick. Amy grew stronger and became impatient with Leslie Knight's strict orders to "take it easy." One day she called Arul and John and asked whether they had seen or heard anything during their nightly patrols.

"Nothing, Amma. All is well."

"Hmm. I feel easier when Jewel's uncle is visible and noisy. All this quiet makes me uneasy. Arul, I know this may sound strange, but I would like you to organize all the *accals* who are strong enough, and all the older girls, to fill every bucket and pot you can find with water from the wells. Place as many as possible by each house with a thatch roof."

What Amma said, the others did. But it took the entire day to gather all the pots not being used, draw water from the wells, and distribute the full pots to the thatch-roofed cottages. John tried to carry a full pot of water on his head like some of the *accals*, but he nearly got a soaking. After that he settled for carrying pots on his shoulders.

When they were done, everyone was tired and aching. "Surely we can sleep tonight," John said, stretching his sore muscles. But Arul insisted that they walk around the wall, just as they had done the previous nights.

John could barely keep his eyes open. But he plodded the length of the east wall from the main gate to God's Garden until he met Azim, who was walking the north wall. Then each went back the way he had come.

Once John thought he heard a branch snap on the other side of the wall, and suddenly all his senses were alert. He barely breathed as he stopped and listened. But even though he stood there for ten minutes, he heard nothing. Finally he started to walk again.

Then out of the corner of his eye he saw it: an arch of flaming light came flying over the wall and landed on the thatch roof of one of the nurseries!

At that same moment, another torch came flying over the wall and landed on the thatch roof of a second nursery. "Fire!" he yelled. "Help! Help! Fire!"

He rushed into the first nursery and shook the form of the *accal* sleeping by the door. "Get out! Everyone out! Fire!" he screamed.

In a split second, girls and *accals* were awake and scooping up the little ones. John grabbed a baby and rushed outside. He handed it to an *accal* who was already holding an infant and trying to gather the others around her. Without stopping to think, he ran over to the second nursery. The fire was now leaping from the roof ten feet into the sky.

He ducked into the dark door. The place was filled with smoke. "Get out! Get out! Fire!" Then holding his breath he felt around the room, shaking the *accal* and older girls. "Get out! Fire!" he hissed. He grabbed two small bundles cuddled up together on a grass mat and stumbled out the door. The *accal* and other girls were coming out now, each holding one or two babies.

John grabbed one of the waterpots they had filled earlier that day and threw it on the burning cottage. It would never be enough! he thought in despair. Then he realized that others had come running and were grabbing the water pots.

Suddenly Jewel was by his side, her face twisted in panic. "*Annachie!* Baba!" she cried, pointing toward the nursery.

What did she mean? *Another baby still in there?* He looked at the flaming roof. No one dared go in the cottage now. He looked around frantically. Where was Arul and Azim? They would know what to do!

Jewel was shaking him. "*Annachie! Annachie!* Baba inside!" John looked into Jewel's face, her eyes wide with fear. Then suddenly she ripped off her scarf, dipped it into a pot of water and gave it to him. *Now,* he thought. *Now or never. God help me.*

Tying the wet scarf around his face, John dove into the door of the cottage. He couldn't see anything. He dropped to his belly and crawled across the floor. He kept feeling grass mats. Empty. Nothing in the corners. The smoke stung his eyes and his lungs hurt when he breathed. Where was the baby? Maybe there was no baby. Maybe . . . wait. Feeling for the storage cupboard, he reached underneath. His hand felt a soft lump. Reaching in with both hands, he pulled out a small child.

Hugging the baby to his chest, John pulled himself along the floor until he found the door. As he stumbled out, he heard someone yell, "His hair's on fire!" and a wall of water hit him full in the face. John was so shocked he just stood there dripping wet.

Someone took the baby from him, and someone else led him over to a tree and pushed him to sit down. For the next few minutes John just sat with his eyes shut, hugging his knees, coughing and choking. The night was filled with shouts, people running, the sounds of flames crackling.

"John, are you all right?" It was Arul. John opened his eyes. His friend was crouching on one knee in front of him.

"The baby," he whispered. He realized he could hardly speak. "Is the baby dead?"

Just then Jewel's face appeared next to Arul. "Baby safe," she said in Tamil. She reached out and touched John's singed hair and smiled. *"Annachie."*

A spasm of coughing gripped John so he could hardly breathe. He looked first at Arul, then Jewel. *"Annachie. Tungachie,"* he whispered. "My brother. My sister."

Then John dropped his head on his arms and cried.

Chapter 8

A Bloody Nose and a Black Eye

As soon as John had arrived back at Kingsway School after the New Year, he had borrowed a bicycle and pedaled over to Woodcock Lodge to ask Mr. Rabur if he could continue his Tamil lessons. The lawyer had heard rumors of the fire and insisted that John sit down and tell him the whole story.

Mr. Rabur listened quietly as John told him about the fire at Dohnavur Fellowship.

"The Lord Jesus protected you, young *sahib*," said the Indian lawyer. "What about the two nurseries? Were they destroyed?"

John nodded. "In spite of all our pots of water! But Amma said that God works all things for good. It was time to replace all the mud-brick and thatch houses with regular brick and tile."

"But rebuilding the cottages would take a lot of money and labor!" said Mr. Rabur. "Did Miss Carmichael appeal for help?"

John shook his head. "That's what I would have done. But Amma has never asked people for money. She believes they should only ask God to supply their needs. So, the women and girls at Dohnavur just started to pray." He smiled sheepishly. "Well, I prayed too, but I grew up with the idea that 'God helps those who help themselves,' so I was rather skeptical. But special money gifts began to come in the mail—from England, the Continent, even America—people who couldn't possibly have heard of the fire that quickly. Not only that, but many of the villagers from Dohnavur, Four Lakes, and even Vallioor showed up to help them rebuild!"

"Amazing!" chuckled Mr. Rabur. "Praise God. But . . . how did your father respond?"

"He was very upset, of course, and wanted us to come right home. He thought the whole situation was getting much too dangerous. Mama wanted to stay and help take care of the babies who had lost their houses, but Amma encouraged her to respect Father's wishes. However, I did stay on for a couple of weeks to help with the building. Somehow it was important. . . ." John hesitated. "You see, I was having nightmares every night about the fire. Mama thought building the new nurseries would help heal the bad memories."

"And?" prompted Mr. Rabur.

John smiled. "It worked. No more nightmares."

"Well! We have used up all our lesson time for today. You need to get back to school before tea or they will send out a search party."

"What about the trial? What's going to happen to Jewel?"

"Patience, young *sahib*," said the lawyer. "These things take time."

"All right," John said. "But I have one more request."

"Yes?"

"Will you call me John instead of 'young *sahib*'? All my teachers at Kingsway call me John."

Mr. Rabur looked very pleased. "Of course. John it is."

John had been assigned to the same dorm room with Torry and Jim again this term, so he braced himself for the inevitable teasing. He gritted his teeth when they made stupid remarks about the Indians and kept his mouth shut about how he'd spent his winter break. But the more he refused to talk about his friends Arul and Jewel, the more Jim and Torry made up their own stories.

"Lover boy must have had a good time with his native girlfriend over winter break," taunted Jim. "He's so secretive."

"Lay off."

"Maybe she lives here in Ooty," said Torry. "John always disappears on Sunday afternoon."

"It's none of your business."

The boys laughed. But one Sunday afternoon as John pedaled back to school on his borrowed bicycle after a language lesson, Jim and Torry were suddenly running alongside.

"So! She lives at Woodcock Lodge! That was some story last term about you going there to see a lawyer."

"Shut up. You don't know what you're talking about."

"Come on, Johnny boy. We're your buddies! You can tell us!"

Jim and Torry badgered him all the way back to Kingsway. Finally John had had enough. "Look, it's no big deal. I'm taking lessons in Tamil from an Indian lawyer, all right? I . . . I'd like to become a lawyer here in India, so I need to know the language."

It just came out, but suddenly John knew it was true. He *was* interested in becoming a lawyer, and he wanted to be a lawyer here in India.

"Oooh, Johnny boy wants to become a swami-lawyer—" Torry started in, but Jim cut him off.

"Really? Say, we don't know any Indian lawyers. Look, John, could you introduce us? I mean, maybe Mister—what's his name? Rabur?—maybe Mr. Rabur could come speak to us over at the school."

John looked at Jim suspiciously. "What do you mean, speak?"

"Well, you know. The Careers Club sponsors speakers telling about different occupations. Mr. Rabur could come and talk about being a lawyer."

"What's the catch?" John wasn't sure he trusted Jim. On the other hand, he thought the boys at

Kingsway should get to know some Indian professionals.

"No catch. Will you ask him?"

And so it was arranged for the first week in March. John was nervous about having Mr. Rabur come to the Careers Club, but Jim's whole attitude seemed to have changed. He stopped calling John "swami-lover" and checked with John several times to be sure Mr. Rabur was coming.

On the scheduled day, John met Mr. Rabur at the gate to Kingsway School and escorted him to the schoolroom where the Careers Club met. John was surprised; the room was packed. As they entered, all voices fell silent. He walked with Mr. Rabur to the front of the room. Something felt wrong, John thought, but he couldn't put his finger on it. Maybe he was just nervous. Then he realized what it was. At Kingsway, the custom was for the boys to stand when a teacher or visiting speaker entered the room. But everyone remained seated.

John brushed the uneasy feeling away. Maybe a club was different than the classroom. He introduced Mr. Rabur, and the Indian lawyer began speaking on law as a profession. He spoke of the many difficult legal issues created by the centuries-old caste system still existing even under the British Crown. He had just begun giving some case studies as examples, when suddenly all the boys rose silently as one person, turned their backs and filed out of the room.

Mr. Rabur stopped uncertainly in mid-sentence. John was astonished. What was happening? He leaped up and grabbed Jim by the arm. "What's happening?" he hissed in Jim's ear. "Why is everyone leaving?"

"Oh, pardon me," Jim said loudly, turning around. "Did we forget to tell you? We double-scheduled by mistake. There's chocolate cake for supper. Really don't want to miss it, you know." And with that Jim sauntered into the hall to a thunder of laughter and clapping.

Something exploded inside John. In three running strides, he tackled Jim and slammed him up against the wall. "You snake!" he cried, and slugged Jim in the jaw as hard as he could with his fist.

"Fight!" someone yelled and arms reached out to grab John. But he tore himself out of their grip and swung at Jim again. But Jim, who was bigger and heavier than John, blocked his arm and threw him to the floor. John felt Jim's fist smash into his nose and

warm blood spurted into his mouth. Then he was jarred by two more blows to his face.

Somewhere in the far distance, nearly drowned out by the shouts and whoops of the boys in the hall, John heard Mr. Rabur commanding, "Stop it! Stop it!" Then he felt himself being hauled up and pushed through the jostling crowd of boys.

"He started it!" he heard Jim yelling behind him. "Did everyone see that? John started it!"

❖ ❖ ❖ ❖

The headmaster restricted John to the dormitory for a month, except for classes and meals. When John tried to explain how rudely Mr. Rabur had been treated by the Careers Club, the headmaster said, "It was just a prank, John. Hardly worth fighting about. Fighting is absolutely against Kingsway rules, and you need to learn a lesson." However, he did move John out of Jim and Torry's room.

John's eye was nearly swollen shut. When the swelling went down, it turned black and blue, causing the other boys to put up their fists mockingly every time he came around. It wasn't so bad until Sunday rolled around and he couldn't go into town for his weekly lesson with Mr. Rabur. John wanted very much to talk with his lawyer friend about what happened, even though Mr. Rabur had said, "Never mind, John. I appreciate your going to bat for me, but it's all right. Fighting doesn't really change people like Jim and his friends."

On Monday a sealed letter was delivered to his room. He unfolded it and looked at the signature. It was from Amy Carmichael.

"Dear John," it said. "We have come to Ooty on . . ."

Ooty! Amma and some of the girls were here in Ooty right now? John felt like bashing his head against the wall of his room. He'd give his right arm to see them, and here he was confined to the dormitory!

He continued reading. "We have come to Ooty on holiday and are staying at Mrs. Hopewell's cottage. March 10 is Jewel's Coming Day. Could you come to help us celebrate? She would very much like to see her *annachie*."

March 10. John looked at his calendar. That would be Thursday. He had no idea what a Coming Day was, but he was going to be there, even if they kicked him out of school.

❖ ❖ ❖ ❖

The door to Mrs. Hopewell's cottage opened in answer to his knock.

"John!" Amy Carmichael said joyously. "You came after all! When we didn't get any reply to our note we thought . . . John! What happened to your eye? And whatever are you wearing?"

John felt silly. He was wearing white leggings, a rumpled tunic, and a *topi* on his head. He told Amy what had happened with Mr. Rabur as briefly as possible. "The only way I could come see you and the girls was to sneak out. I talked one of the Muslim boys who works in the kitchen to loan me some clothes, so . . . here I am!"

"For all the world looking like a pagan! And acting like one, too!" Miss Carmichael said, shaking her head. "Fighting, indeed. Well, come on out to the garden. The girls are having a party."

She led John through the lovely English cottage and through the double glass doors that led into the garden. The girls in their colorful saris were tossing a ball back and forth, trying to keep it 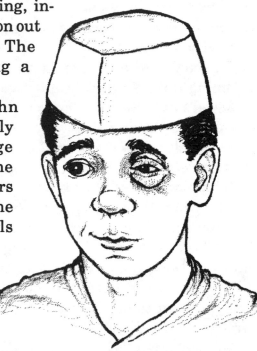 away from Jewel, who was dancing about in the center.

John stared. Jewel's head was wreathed in flowers and her dark hair hung loosely about her shoulders. She was wearing a sky blue sari with silver edges and a necklace of flowers hung about her neck. He realized that in a year she had grown from a twelve-year-old girl-child to a thirteen-year-old young woman.

Jewel caught the ball and turned to show Amy. *"Annachie!"* she cried when she saw John. All the girls came running, and they all made clucking noises when they saw John's black eye. Amy shooed them away and soon had them shrieking with laughter in a game of Follow the Leader.

"You are hurt?" Jewel said to John soberly in Tamil. John felt a thrill, realizing he could understand her.

He shook his head. "I'm all right now. But what is a Coming Day? Your birthday?"

Jewel's eyes lit up. "Don't you remember? March 10—Jewel's Coming Day!"

Suddenly it dawned on John. It was exactly a year ago that Jewel had come pounding on the gate of Dohnavur crying, "Refuge!"

Amy Carmichael plopped down beside the English boy and Indian girl. "I'm getting too old for games!" she wheezed. Then giving Jewel a hug, she said, "At Dohnavur we don't always know when a child was born. But we do know the glad day God brought them to us. So instead of birthdays we celebrate Coming Days!"

John grinned. "Then I guess it's my Coming Day, too! Come on, Jewel, let's go play Follow the Leader!"

The party lasted into the twilight. They laughed and sang, and ate wonderful treats Amy had prepared for the occasion. John hated to leave, for he knew that he wouldn't be able to sneak out again—if he hadn't been discovered already. Before he left, he had a talk with Amy Carmichael.

"Amma," he said, as they stood on the stoop in front of Mrs. Hopewell's cottage, "would you pray for me?" The words sounded strange to John. In all his fifteen years he had never asked anyone to pray for him before. "I have so many feelings about India and its people—people like Arul and Jewel and the other girls and Mr. Rabur. But I get so angry at people like Jim and Torry and others. And I feel confused when I'm with my father. He's a good magistrate, and is careful to apply the law justly. I admire him. But sometimes . . ." John stared into the deepening twilight at the moon rising above the Nilgiri hills. He didn't know how to say that he felt lonely—especially here at school, but also in Palamcottah. Everywhere except Dohnavur.

Amy Carmichael walked him to the cottage gate. She nodded. "I will pray, dear John." She clasped both his hands in hers. "Go in peace, my son. Someday, I know, you will do great things for God and for India."

As he trotted off into the darkness, he heard her call out after him, "But no more fighting!"

Chapter 9

On Trial

JOHN PAID A COUPLE RUPEES to the Muslim boy in the school kitchen for the leggings and tunic and kept them. The clothes had helped him out once; who knew when he might need them again?

By October of that year, 1910, John had completed his public school education at Kingsway School for Boys. After graduation, Sanford Knight began making preparations to send his sixteen-year-old son back to England for further education.

"But, Father," John reasoned, "you know I'm interested in law. I'd like to observe some of the court proceedings in Palamcottah—especially now that you are the senior magistrate. I know I would learn a lot."

Sanford Knight rubbed his chin thoughtfully.

"And besides," John went on, "if I wait to begin college until next June, mother and I can spend Christmas with you here."

"He's right, Sanford." Leslie Knight eagerly embraced the idea. "Once John goes back to England, visits will be few and far between. Let's enjoy a few more months together before being separated."

"I know I'm in trouble when you both gang up on me," Mr. Knight smiled, shaking his head. "All right. We'll wait until March to book passage on a ship. Leslie, it's been two years since you've been home to England. Why don't you travel with John, see your family in Brighton, and get him settled in school? That way you'll miss the monsoon season altogether."

John breathed a sigh of relief. The family discussion had gone just the way he wanted. But he had other reasons for wanting to stay. The trial date to decide Jewel's fate had been set for September 3, then postponed to October 8, then October 28, and now Mr. Rabur had just informed him that it had been set back to December 21.

Leslie Knight guessed what was going on in John's head. "This could be very difficult, John," she said gently when they were alone. "The case may very likely end up in your father's court, meaning he will have to rule in the case."

John hadn't thought of that. "But Father is just; he will surely rule in Dohnavur's favor."

"Yes, your father is just. But we—you and I—see this situation from a very personal viewpoint. Your father sees it as an issue of law and local tradition."

A visit to Dohnavur in early December was a joyous reunion with Amy Carmichael, Arul, Jewel, and the others. John was amazed at the nurseries and other new buildings with their sloping red-tile roofs. "You not only rebuilt the old ones," he said, "you've built some new ones."

"God keeps sending us little Lotus Buds." Amy smiled. "And someday God will send us men workers—and then we will open our doors to little boys whose families sell them to the temples and pagan acting groups."

While John was at Dohnavur, Amy received word from Mr. Rabur that the trial had been postponed once again—indefinitely.

Christmas passed, then the New Year, then February. No new trial date had been set. John's heart sank. He and his mother had tickets sailing from Colombo, Ceylon, the big island off the tip of southern India, on March 24. How could he go to England without knowing what would happen to Jewel?

John was in this frame of mind when he came frowning into the courtyard in Palamcottah one day in early March, only to discover that his mother had a guest.

"John!" she called. "Come meet my old school chum, Mabel Beath. Mabel has heard all about Dohnavur Fellowship in my letters and wants very much to visit there." Leslie Knight turned back to her friend. "All visitors to Dohnavur somehow become volunteers, however, so be warned!" she laughed. Then her smile faded. "The situation with the girl named Jewel is very serious. Miss Carmichael has risked prison several times standing up to the uncle's claims on the girl."

John didn't want to hear any more. He felt too upset. But in the next few days he came to like Mabel Beath despite his bad mood. The motherly lady had a way of coaxing a laugh out of him, and she seemed genuinely interested in Jewel's story.

Mabel Beath left for Dohnavur on the same day John and his mother took the train for the coast. Both mother and son gave letters of farewell to Mabel to deliver to their friends at Dohnavur Fellowship.

"Take care of your mother, John," Sanford Knight said, firmly gripping John's hand. "You shouldn't have any trouble. There's a ferry across the gulf, then another train will take you to Colombo. I have reserved rooms in a hotel there for you until the ship sails."

John stared out the compartment window as the train rattled through the countryside. Oxen were plowing up rice fields; farmers were setting out new shoots. Women beat clothes on rocks in the rivers; *mahoots* sat on the heads of their elephants as the beasts pulled logs out of the forests or paraded through the villages in temple dress.

He was leaving India. Would he ever see Arul and Jewel and Amma again?

❖ ❖ ❖

A telegram was waiting for them at the hotel in Colombo. It was from Mr. Rabur, the lawyer.

TRIAL SET FOR MARCH 27 *STOP* PRAY FOR US *STOP* GOD'S WILL BE DONE *STOP*

John and his mother stared at each other.

"I can't believe this!" John said furiously. He kicked one of their bags sitting on the floor.

"Maybe it's for the best," his mother started to say.

"No, it's not!" John interrupted. "I can't leave India without knowing what's happening. It'll be months before we hear. . . . Where's that sailing schedule."

John ran a finger down the sailing dates.

"Mama," he said, straightening up. "This is the biggest favor I'm ever going to ask of you. Don't get on the ship. There's another ship that sails in two weeks. We'll take that one."

"But, John! The tickets . . . your father . . . what are you going to do?"

"I'm going back to Palamcottah. I'm going to be there for that trial!"

❖ ❖ ❖ ❖

John only had four days to get back to Palamcottah. Without reservations, he ended up going third class most of the way. Eight to ten people were crammed in each compartment, some sitting on the sleeping berths overhead. The Indians in third class stared at this English boy traveling by himself. They stared even more when he said, "May I sit down?" or "When is the next train?" in Tamil.

Several times an Indian woman, carrying food for her family in a woven basket and seeing he had none, would share some rice or curry with him. But at least twice he felt stealthy fingers reaching into his pockets; he was glad the money his mother had given him was tucked safely in a pouch under his shirt.

The first night he slept very little. The heat, strong body odor, and fear of being robbed kept him awake. But by the second day he was so exhausted he fell asleep on the floor of a train station, using the small bag of clothes he was carrying as a pillow.

As the train wheels clicked loudly between towns, John kept praying, "O God, please let me get there on time."

John was in a daze when he got off the train in

Palamcottah at noon on Monday. It was March 27. But was he in time for the trial?

He went straight to the courthouse and made his way up into the crowded gallery where the public was allowed to watch court proceedings. He stationed himself as close to the railing as he could, using a rather fat man as a shield, and looked down.

Amy Carmichael and Mr. Rabur sat at a table on one side of the courtroom. Jewel's uncle and his lawyer sat on the other side. John stretched his neck. Jewel was nowhere to be seen. *Where could she be?* he wondered.

Back at Dohnavur? Then he heard a familiar voice say, "Will the clerk please read the judgment?"

It was his father, sitting on the judge's bench.

John frowned. The judgment already? He had missed all the arguments! What had happened? Was it going well for Jewel staying at Dohnavur or not?

An Indian clerk stood up and began reading from several pages. John strained to hear, but couldn't catch what all the complex, legal language meant. Then after several minutes the clerk read something that caused a stir in the gallery.

"Quiet!" said Sanford Knight, banging his gavel. "Will the clerk read the judgment once more?"

The clerk raised his voice. "The court hereby orders Amy Carmichael, of Dohnavur Fellowship, to surrender the child in question to her legal guardian by April 4, and to pay all court costs of these proceedings."

Pandemonium broke out in the gallery, with cheers, shaking fists, hugs and laughter. John realized he was standing in the midst of the uncle's relatives and friends. But he felt as though someone had slugged him in the stomach. Jewel had to go back to her uncle within a week, then be forced into a marriage she didn't want?

On the main floor the uncle was vigorously pumping his lawyer's hand up and down. John's gaze shifted to Amy Carmichael who sat quietly on the other side of the room. Her hands were folded on the table in front of her, her face tilted slightly up and her eyes closed. Was she praying? Then John saw her smile; a look of triumphant peace and joy seemed to radiate from her face.

The crowd was moving out of the gallery, and John let it carry him down the stairs and outside. Should he go in and see Amy and Mr. Rabur? What about his father? But he felt numb, incapable of making a decision or talking to anyone. Instead, he found himself walking back toward his father's house, his bag of clothes slung over his shoulder.

As he walked into the courtyard through the small gate at the rear of the house, John had no idea what he was going to do. His bicycle, the one Azim had fixed up for him, was leaning against the cookhouse, a one-room cottage separate from the main house where all the cooking was done.

John stared at the bicycle. He looked around; no one had seen him yet. Then, suddenly, he knew what he had to do.

Chapter 10

Disappeared!

JOHN PEEKED INTO the cookhouse. Empty. He slipped inside, rummaged through his bag and pulled out the leggings, tunic, and topi. Taking off his shirt, shorts, and shoes, he put on the native clothes. Then he noticed his white hands and feet, and his heart sank. Wait . . . he snatched up a coffeepot and looked inside. There was a thick brown paste at the bottom; the cook often left the pot on the fire too long. He smeared the thick coffee on his hands. They stained a nice nut brown. Perfect! He quickly covered all his exposed skin, remembering at the last minute to do his ears and the back of his neck.

The courtyard was still empty. The servants often rested during the hottest part of the day, espe-

cially when the family wasn't at home. John picked up the bicycle, stuffed his bag in the basket, and wheeled it out the gate.

The road to Dohnavur had the usual traffic: farmers in their slow-moving ox carts, women walking with pots on their heads, a few bicycles, a string of donkeys with their drivers. But John barely noticed. At first he pedaled furiously, but then realized he had twenty miles to cover and finally settled into a steady pace.

The shock of the court judgment wore off and anger rose in its place. How could his father rule against Jewel? *How could he!* Didn't he realize what returning Jewel to her uncle would mean? A child bride . . . John's stomach turned at the thought of Jewel being forced to go through a pagan wedding ceremony and becoming the wife of an old man who didn't even love her. She was only fourteen!

Well. He was *annachie*, Jewel's "older brother." And he wasn't going to let it happen.

What he was going to do once he got to Dohnavur, he had no idea. But something inside drove him on. He had to let them know what the court judgment was. They had to save her.

He turned off the main road at Four Lakes and headed for the village of Dohnavur. Only six miles to go. In Dohnavur he spun through the dirt streets, scattering chickens that got in his way. Finally he could see the compound wall and main gate of Dohnavur Fellowship.

John got off his bike, and suddenly his legs felt wobbly. Four exhausting days of train travel with little sleep and a twenty-mile bicycle ride was catching up with him. He pushed the bike to the side of the road and sat down, head between his knees, chest heaving.

He sat for some time, trying to catch his breath, when a shadow fell over him.

"Are you ill?" said a gentle woman's voice.

John looked up. "Miss Beath?" he said. It was his mother's friend, the one who had come to visit Dohnavur.

"Wha—who are you? How do you know my name?"

John struggled to his feet. "It's me—John Knight."

"My word!" the lady exclaimed, then started to laugh. "I never would have guessed. But I thought you and your mother—"

"Miss Beath! I can't explain it all now. But the court—my father—ruled against Dohnavur. Jewel must be returned to her uncle next week!"

"No! Oh, dear God."

"I must tell Jewel, and Arul, and the *accals*. It's urgent!" John picked up his bike and started for the gate.

"John, wait!" Mabel Beath put her hand on the boy's shoulder. "Does anyone know you are here? Does your father? Or Miss Carmichael?"

"No . . . I only got back to Palamcottah this morning. No one saw me at the trial."

"Then no one here must see you, either."

"Why?"

"Come, let's talk."

Reluctantly, John hid his bicycle in some bushes and walked with Miss Beath into the brush and a stand of tamarind trees where they couldn't be seen from the road.

"When I came to Dohnavur," said Miss Beath, "my spirit immediately felt at one with Amy Carmichael and her work here. I understood when she promised Jewel that, whatever happened, she would not return her against her will to her uncle. Jewel has entrusted her life to us; Amma could not fail her."

John nodded. Yes, he understood that, too.

"The night before Miss Carmichael left for court, she came to me and looked into my eyes," Miss Beath continued. "'If everything fails,' Amma said, 'are you willing to help save Jewel?' 'Yes,' I replied. 'Even if it means seven years in prison?' she asked. Again I said yes."

They had stopped walking and just stood looking at each other, the dusty boy dressed in Muslim clothes and the middle-aged English woman.

"I was walking outside the wall praying when I saw you," the woman said. "And now I know what we must do. *But we must do it alone!* No one must know—not Arul or Miss Carmichael or any of the others—because they will be questioned. It will look like they have disobeyed the court judgment. But if they know nothing, if Jewel has simply disappeared . . ."

❖ ❖ ❖ ❖

"Stupid oxen!" muttered John as he pulled at their halters and tried to get the bandy turned around. Miss Beath had told him to come to this side gate after dark and wait.

When the oxen were finally turned around and facing toward the village, John climbed up into the bandy. "Wait how long?" he wondered.

He had hidden in the bushes until dusk, as Miss Beath instructed. Once he fell into a deep sleep and awoke with hunger pangs gnawing at his stomach. Why hadn't he grabbed some food from the cookhouse back in Palamcottah?

When darkness settled, he had trotted into the village looking for a bandy to rent. John hoped the darkness would help cover his disguise. He was careful to speak only Tamil, but he had a hard time convincing the bandy owner that he needed the oxen and bandy *without* a driver.

A monkey screeched nearby, and for a few minutes there was a general hubbub out in the brush. But he heard nothing from inside the compound walls. What was happening in there?

It was so hard to sit outside the compound, knowing Arul was inside. How he wished he could talk to the older boy! He wanted to see him again, tell him all about getting the telegram and the crazy train trip back to Palamcottah . . . the trial . . . the furious ride by bicycle all the way to Dohnavur. What would Arul think of Miss Beath's idea? John wished Arul could come with them! Arul would know what to do. Arul could . . . no, Miss Beath was right. Arul must not know anything so he could honestly say, "I don't know," if the police questioned him.

Thinking of the trial made John feel angry all over again. But what was it that Miss Beath had said just before she left him in the brush?

"John, don't be angry with your father. He did what he thought was right according to the law. I'm sure Amma is not angry; she knew the ruling might not be in her favor. If the judgment went against her, she intended to stay and appeal, to continue to fight for Jewel. And now we must do what seems right to save Jewel. Be very certain of that, John. If a Christian breaks the law to honor Christ, that person must also be willing to suffer the consequences."

John's thoughts were interrupted by a creaking

sound. The gate was opening. Instantly all John's senses were alert. A young boy stepped through the gate and looked around uncertainly. The gate closed behind him.

John was confused. He was supposed to wait for Jewel. Was it Arul? No, the boy was much too young.

The boy, who was carrying several small bundles, saw the bandy and scurried across the road toward John. "*Annachie?*" said a familiar voice in Tamil. "You have come for me?"

John stared in disbelief. *It was Jewel!*

"But your hair—it is all cut off," stammered John, saying the first thing that popped into his mind.

"And you look like an Indian boy!" said Jewel,

scrambling into the back of the bandy. She handed John one of the bundles. "Food for you. Mabel friend says you are very hungry." She pointed at the other bundles. "More food for the journey."

John smacked the whip on the backs of the oxen until they started moving down the road, then opened the bundle. He shoveled handfuls of the warm vegetable-and-rice curry into his mouth until his stomach was satisfied. Then he looked back into the bandy.

Jewel was sitting at the opening in the rear, looking back toward Dohnavur Fellowship, already hidden among the trees. "Goodbye, Amma," he heard her whisper in Tamil. "Goodbye, Arul *annachie*. Goodbye, sister friends. Goodbye, *babas*. Goodbye, Mabel friend."

Suddenly John felt very alone. He shivered, even though the March evening was hot and still. Jewel was now in his care. No one was coming with them; no one except Mabel Beath even knew where he was—and she was leaving Dohnavur before it was discovered that Jewel was gone.

"Oh, God!" he cried out silently. "Help us!"

Jewel crawled up beside him at the front of the bandy. "*Annachie*, where are we going?"

John glanced at the girl beside him, hair cut short and dressed like a boy. Then he looked at his own coffee-stained hands, dark against the white leggings he wore. Then he looked at the dark road that stretched out in front of them. Two "Indian boys" on their way to . . .

"Ceylon," he said. "We're going to Ceylon."

Chapter 11

Discovered

JOHN KEPT THE OXEN traveling east by back roads all through the night while Jewel slept in the back of the bandy. Toward morning they came to a village called Saltan's Tank, where they found a boy who was willing to return the bandy to the village of Dohnavur for a few rupees. But by this time John could hardly keep his eyes open, so he lay down to sleep under a tree just outside the village while Jewel kept watch.

In the late afternoon, the two young people set off on foot for the Town of Siva's Son, a Hindu town with a large temple right on the eastern coast of southern India. They covered the fifteen miles in four hours. As they wandered through the streets of the town at dusk, John felt anxious—what were they going to do?

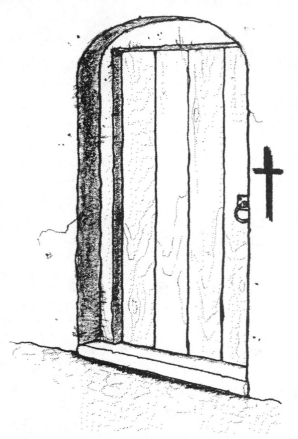

"*Annachie,* look!" said Jewel. The girl was pointing to a simple house with a Christian cross painted on the wall beside the door. With his heart beating fast, John knocked at the door. It was opened by a woman who was not wearing the Hindu red dot on her forehead.

John pointed to the cross, then to themselves. "We are Jesus believers," he said in Tamil.

The woman smiled. "Come in, come in." She called to someone who sat outside behind the house in a small courtyard. "Pastor husband, two boys to see you."

A smiling Indian gentleman greeted them with the customary salaam; John and Jewel returned the greeting. "What do you need?" the man asked kindly in Tamil.

"We are going to Ceylon to find my mother," John said truthfully. The rest of the story did not need to be told. "But we need food and a place to sleep."

The man looked at them silently for what seemed a long time. Finally he smiled. "You boys are welcome to what we have."

They spent the night with the man and his wife, who had a small congregation of five Christian believers in the Town of Siva's Son. John was grateful that they did not ask many questions, but he worried that his disguise did not hold up under close scrutiny. In the morning the woman packed some more food in their bundle, but the man was nowhere to be seen.

"Wait. He will come," said the wife.

John was anxious to be on their way, but they waited. Soon the man arrived with a bandy and two oxen. "I will drive you as far as Tuticorin," he said, naming the next largest town about twenty miles up the coast. "There other Christians will help you."

John looked uncertainly at Jewel. A ride and someone to help them on their way would be wonderful. He hadn't said anything to Jewel, but he was worried about robbers on the road and an escort would provide some safety. On the other hand, maybe their greatest safety lay in keeping to themselves. If they got too familiar with people—even helpful ones—someone would soon guess they were not two Indian boys at all.

But the pastor was waiting. So John said, "Thank you," and gave Jewel a hand up into the wagon bed.

In Tuticorin, the pastor took them to the house of another Christian couple. He spoke privately with the man and woman, who nodded, glancing at John and Jewel from time to time.

Before he left, the pastor took John aside. "Trust our friends. Do not go alone until you get to the train. No questions will be asked. But," and the man smiled, "let the woman help you be an Indian boy."

John was startled. What did he mean? But the man salaamed and then waved goodbye, slapping the rumps of the oxen as the wagon headed back down the road to the Town of Siva's Son.

He soon found out. Jewel came to him with a strange brown paste and a length of white cloth. "Woman friend says to help you be an Indian boy," she said, grinning at him. She made him take off the tunic, while she rubbed the brown paste all over his chest, back, arms and hands, neck and face. John did his own feet and legs. Then Jewel wound the white cloth around his hair, making a small, neat turban.

John felt humiliated. How many people had seen through his hasty disguise? But Jewel looked at him approvingly. Maybe it was better now.

John and Jewel were taken to the next town, then the next, and each time handed over to local Christians. Very few questions were asked and they said little, only that they were on their way to Ceylon to find "mother." Their food bundle was refilled several times, and when they arrived at the train station that would take them to the Ceylon ferry, their stomachs were full.

On an impulse John bought a postcard, addressed it to Amy Carmichael in care of Dohnavur Fellowship, turned it over and printed in English: "The eyes of the Lord run to and fro throughout the whole earth, to show Himself strong in behalf of them whose heart is perfect toward Him." It was one of Amma's favorite Bible verses; he had heard her quote it many times when calming the fears of the little ones. He left the card unsigned. No one must know who wrote it, or why. But would Amma read between the lines, that Jewel was safe?

Two tickets to Colombo used the last of John's money strapped in the pouch around his waist. As he and Jewel collapsed on the hard bench in a third-class compartment, a strange feeling of weariness and peace seemed to consume his whole body. He had no idea what they would do once they got to Colombo. But hadn't God been with them each step of the way ever since they left Dohnavur Fellowship at night in the bandy? God would provide for Jewel . . . somehow.

✧ ✧ ✧ ✧

The hotel room door opened and Leslie Knight stood looking at the two Indian boys with a strange, confused look on her face. Her hair was mussed and her face was strained.

"Mother! It's me—and Jewel."

Mrs. Knight's eyes widened and her mouth fell open. Reaching out, she pulled them into the room and shut the door. "John! Jewel! Oh, thank God!" she cried, clasping both of them to her, crying and laughing at the same time.

"Whatever in the world!" she finally gasped, holding them at arm's length and shaking her head. "I have been frantic with worry. When ten days went by and I still hadn't heard from you . . ." Her eyes filled with tears. "Tell me! Tell me everything!"

So John told the whole story from start to finish, while Jewel snuggled in the comfort of Leslie Knight's arm around her. His mother wouldn't let him leave out any detail. Finally she said, "But Amy Carmichael has no idea where Jewel is or who took her?"

"No. Miss Beath said no one at Dohnavur should know for their own protection."

Mrs. Knight was silent for a long time. Finally she said, "John, you know I don't like doing anything behind your father's back. I cabled him that we had an unexpected delay and would get the next ship. I told him not to worry, that we would enjoy our enforced holiday."

John felt alarmed. Had his mother's cable given them away? "Did he . . . ?"

"I got a reply yesterday. He sent money to help cover our additional expenses and expressed regret that he could not join us due to the number of court cases there in Palamcottah."

John breathed a sigh of relief. So far so good.

But Leslie Knight frowned. "Now that Jewel is here, what are we going to do? We can't stay in Ceylon indefinitely—and we can't leave Jewel here alone!"

Mother and son decided that John should scrub off the brown stain and resume his own identity, but that Jewel should stay hidden in the hotel room. Leslie Knight had meals sent up, and either she or John stayed with Jewel at all times.

In the next few days they discussed various plans: find a Christian church in Colombo and ask for protection for Jewel; take Jewel with them to England; send John back to England as planned, but Mrs. Knight would stay and continue looking for a safe place for Jewel. Each plan, however, had problems.

Nonetheless, John went down to the ship to see if there were any more tickets available for the next voyage. As he stood in the line, he noticed a large Englishman looking at him closely. John pretended not to notice. When it was his turn, he started to ask about another ticket, but noticed that the big man was standing close enough to hear his request. Abruptly John said, "I've changed my mind," and left the line.

He tried again the next day, but was told that there was now a waiting list. Did he want to add a name to the list in case someone canceled? John shook his head. Frustrated, he walked back to the hotel. As he entered the lobby, he saw the big Englishman talking to one of the Indian servants. He ducked behind some of the potted palms and hurried up the stairs to their room.

"What's the matter?" said his mother as he entered out of breath.

"I'm not sure. But there's a man—English—I

think he's been following me."

"Oh, surely not—" began Mrs. Knight.

Just then there was a knock at the door.

"Jewel!" John hissed. "Quickly! Hide!"

John grabbed Jewel's hand and pulled her into the sleeping room she and his mother shared. He pushed her under the bed—a real English bed with a ruffle covering the mattress and legs—then returned to the other room just as he heard his mother open the door.

A man's deep voice said, "Mrs. Knight? My name is Handley Bird, formerly of England, now God's servant in southern India. I believe you have a little bird who has fallen from its nest and needs safekeeping?"

Reverend Handley Bird wore a rumpled white suit and a straw hat, which he twisted in his hands as he talked. Leslie Knight had ordered tea from the hotel and invited the caller to sit. John stood off to the side as his mother poured the tea. Was he a friend or an enemy?

"What is it you want, Reverend Bird?" asked Mrs. Knight, handing the visitor a cup.

The man smiled. He had ruddy cheeks and white bushy eyebrows that twitched up and down as he talked. "I was on holiday in Ooty when I ran into an old friend of my wife's, a Miss Amy Carmichael. She had come to Ooty to confer with her lawyer, a Mr. Rabur—I believe you know him?" The man looked at John.

John nodded slightly.

"She is very concerned over the plight of a girl named Jewel, who has disappeared. After telling me the story, and knowing I was on holiday, she asked for my help in locating her. I said I would, with all my heart."

"But why did you come to us?" John demanded. "Why do you think she is here?"

"After hearing as much as I could from Miss Carmichael and Mr. Rabur, I made a trip to Palamcottah to talk to the judge in the case—your husband, I believe, Mrs. Knight."

"That's right."

"I must admit I did not tell him I was acting on Miss Carmichael's behalf! In fact, Jewel's case only happened to come up as we talked about other legal matters of interest affecting the Tinnevelly District. While I was there a telegram arrived—"

"My telegram?" asked Mrs. Knight.

"Yes. Only later, as I was mulling over the whole affair, did the pieces seem to fall in place. A sailing date delayed . . . a girl disappears. Miss Mabel Beath, who left Dohnavur Fellowship on the day of the trial, was followed, but the girl was not found. Let me assure you that I told no one of my hunch— not even Miss Carmichael. After all, I knew nothing for sure."

"How do we know you are here as Miss Carmichael's friend?" John challenged. "Why should we trust you?"

"John . . ." reproved his mother gently.

"It is all right, madam," said Reverend Bird. "If this young man has spirited away our little bird through untold adventures and hardships, he has a right to know whom he should trust."

The stocky man drew a postcard from his coat pocket and handed it to Mrs. Knight. "Miss Carmichael gave me this."

John's mother took the postcard. "Why, John, this is your handwriting!"

"Ah!" said the man. He seemed satisfied.

John walked over to his mother and took the

card. "I only wanted to let Miss Carmichael know that Jewel was safe. I . . . I didn't mean to leave a trail that could be traced."

"Oh, my boy, you have done a very good job covering your tracks. To this day no one suspects— except me. And I assure you I am a friend, and have promised Miss Carmichael I will not rest until Jewel is safely out of the country."

"Out of the country?" John and his mother said together.

"Yes. China. I have reason to believe that Jewel's relatives have hired detectives to find her. They will stop at nothing to get her back. She is not safe here— it is only a matter of time before they follow everyone who has had anything to do with Jewel. I believe Jewel and I must leave immediately—today. I will deliver her to missionary friends in China where she can stay until she comes of age. Then she can inherit her father's land and choose to marry whom she will."

Mrs. Knight and John stared at Reverend Bird in stunned silence. It was all happening so fast.

"Er, by the way, where is the little bird?" the missionary asked.

"Oh, no! Jewel!" John remembered. He ran into the sleeping room and pulled Jewel out from under the bed.

"*Annachie* forgot Jewel," the girl pouted.

John led her into the other room. The bushy white eyebrows raised, and John realized Jewel did not look like a girl with her hair cut short and still wearing the boy's leggings and tunic. In halting Tamil, John tried to explain to Jewel what Reverend Bird had told them, and that he wanted to take her to China to keep her safe from her uncle.

Jewel looked at the man with her dark, trusting eyes. "If Amma sent Bird man to take care of Jewel, then I will go," she said in Tamil. She turned to John and Mrs. Knight. "If *annachie* and Leslie friend say Bird man is Amma's friend, then I will go."

Mrs. Knight, not understanding, looked at John for help.

John took Jewel's hands in his own and swallowed hard. "Yes, *tungachie*, sister. The Bird man is your friend. You must go."

Chapter 12

The Bride of Dohnavur

ALONE HORSEMAN rode south on the road from Palamcottah toward Dohnavur. It had been six years since John Knight had stood on the train station platform in Colombo, Ceylon, waving goodbye to the Indian girl he knew as Jewel. The young man, now twenty-two, could still remember the scene as if it had been yesterday: Jewel, her hair chopped short, leaning out the train window, smiling and crying at the same time; behind her, the ruddy face and bushy eyebrows of Reverend Handley Bird.

The rider was lost in his thoughts, and the horse veered around a slow-moving ox cart, keeping up a steady trot. John knew Reverend Bird and Jewel made it safely to China after a dangerous journey that took several months. He had practically memorized the letter he had received from Amy Carmichael in late fall that year after he had entered Oxford . . .

. . . Reverend Bird just disappeared and I had no idea what was happening. Then in October I received a letter from China. Our precious Jewel is safe! I have since heard the whole story, and I am astounded at the great risks you took to save her. But I thank you, John, from the bottom of my heart.

Waiting to hear for so many months with no word about Jewel's fate was a real challenge of faith for me. But even when the judgment was pronounced against us that day in court, the Lord gave me an overwhelming sense of victory! Jewel belonged to Him! . . .

Since that time, John had heard little news. He spent the next six years studying law at Oxford near London. His mother, after getting him settled at school, had returned to India to be with his father. But after a severe illness brought on by drinking some unboiled water, she never fully regained her strength. Eventually both Leslie and Sanford Knight had returned to England.

The meeting with his father had been strained at first. Once Jewel was safely away, Leslie Knight had felt compelled to tell her husband of their role in the affair. John knew his father was angry. After all, the magistrate's son had deliberately interfered with a ruling of the court!

John had been angry with his father, too. The court judgment had seemed so heartless! So calloused!

But on one of John's visits home from the university, Sanford Knight had called him into the library. "Son," he said, clearing his throat, "your mother and I have talked about what happened many times. I can accept that you did what you thought you had to do. Even though I was angry when I discovered you had helped Jewel disappear, I have to admit I felt somewhat relieved. I ruled as I thought right based on the laws that concern India's family system and religious traditions—but I did not enjoy returning Jewel to her uncle."

John accepted his father's outstretched hand. Maybe father and son could respect, if not agree with, the action taken by the other.

✧ ✧ ✧ ✧

The young man on horseback reached for the canteen hanging from the saddle, unscrewed the cap and drank. When he told his mother that he was returning to India, she was quick to say, "Don't forget to boil the water!"

He chuckled; his horse's ears twisted backward to catch the sound. That was India, all right: everything one took for granted in England—clean water, soft beds, a proper roof over your head—was a challenge in India.

As he rode into Four Lakes, John reined in his

horse at a food stall in the marketplace and bought two mangoes and some freshly baked flat bread for his lunch. Mounting once more, he turned his horse toward Dohnavur.

A feeling of excitement grew as John kicked the horse into an easy canter for the last few miles. Through the six long years he had been away, John had never once lost sight of his goal: to return to India and be an advocate for the people. But when he arrived, the first thing he had done was buy a good horse and set out for Dohnavur Fellowship. Before anything else he wanted to see his friends.

John slowed his horse to a trot. There was the village . . . cows creating traffic jams in the middle of the street, as usual . . . children running after him . . . spicy smells rising from the cooking fires in front of the mud houses. And there, through the trees, the mud-brick walls of Dohnavur Fellowship. John's heart seemed to beat faster.

Dismounting, the young man pulled the bell on the gate.

After a few minutes, the gate swung open. John stared at the familiar man who stood before him.

"Azim!" he cried. "What in the world are you doing here!"

His father's former Indian servant looked startled.

"It's me—John Knight!"

The man's eyes lit up. "Yes, yes! Young *sahib*." And Azim pressed his hands together in the familiar *salaam*.

John shook his head and laughed. "No, not *sahib*," he said. "We are friends! John and Azim!"

John led his horse into the compound, following Azim to the main house. What was Azim doing here? Why didn't Arul open the gate? Maybe he should have written that he was coming. But he wanted to surprise Arul and Miss Carmichael.

As he tied his horse to a nearby tree, John noticed that something seemed to be happening. Brightly colored streamers fluttered from the porch roof. Older girls, dressed in their colorful skirts and scarves, were setting baskets of freshly picked flowers from the gardens around the yard. Groups of younger girls sat on blankets under the trees, stringing jasmine flowers into necklaces and long ropes. Oil-soaked rags had been tied on thick sticks and stuck in the ground, making a line of unlit torches all the way from the gate to the house.

John stood looking around, somewhat bewildered, then he heard his name. "John! John Knight! I can't believe it!" Amy Carmichael came whirling out of the house and before he realized what was happening, had thrown her arms around him in a motherly hug.

The next moment she was holding him at arm's length. "Let me look at you. You have grown up into a proper young man! What a wonderful surprise." And she gave him another hug.

John was so happy to see her he couldn't even say anything.

"But why didn't you write that you were coming? What are you doing back in India? How long are you staying?"

John had to laugh at her long list of questions. But there was something he had to know first.

"Where is Arul? I came to see you—and Arul."

Her eyes widened. "You don't know? No . . . of course you don't. Oh, John, Arul isn't here!"

Disappointment rose in John's throat. Not here? He had come all the way to Dohnavur and Arul was not here?

"But . . . where—?" he began.

"Time for that later," said Miss Carmichael briskly. She took him by the arm and bustled him into the house. "The others will want to see you."

The faithful Indian staff women were decorating the inside of the house as well. Each one expressed surprise and delight upon seeing John, after which there was much whispering among the women.

"And Azim?" he managed to ask as she propelled him out the door once more.

"Oh, yes, Azim! When your mother and father left Palamcottah, Azim had no employment. He had been so helpful when he came with you and your mother that I asked if he would like to come and work for

Dohnavur. He gladly accepted. And," she lowered her voice in a secretive tone, "he is *almost* convinced that all men are brothers, just as Jesus taught, in spite of his long dedication to the caste system." The two laughed.

Amy took him around to the groups of children and introduced him. Some of the older girls remembered him, lowered their eyes shyly, and bent their heads in gentle salaams. To the younger ones, Amy said, "Little Lotus Buds, this is John—Jewel's *annachie*, as I have told you in the stories."

Lots of giggles and finger pointing came from the wiggly bundles on the blankets.

John worked up his courage as Amy took him back to sit on the porch and got him something cool to drink.

"What has happened to Jewel?" he asked. "Has she returned? Have you seen her?"

Amy's mouth twitched. Was she about to cry—or smile? He couldn't tell which.

"No," Amy said. "No, I have not seen Jewel since the day I left her to go to court that fateful day six years ago."

John was silent. He watched the streamers flutter in the slight breeze. Something strange was going on. Arul was not here . . . Amma seemed reluctant to talk about him, or Jewel. Had something bad happened? And yet, what about the streamers and flowers? On the other hand, he remembered Arul telling him that funerals at Dohnavur were great celebrations as a much-loved child or *accal* moved from this life into eternal life with Jesus.

"You look like you are getting ready for a celebration," he hinted finally.

Amy nodded, but said nothing. Then suddenly she jumped up. "Well! I have things I need to do. Just sit here and rest. I am sure you are tired after your journey. We will talk again when I am done with my duties. We have so much catching up to do!"

She disappeared into the house. In a few minutes, John heard much commotion and laughter inside.

He got up and paced the length of the porch. His riding boots thumped on the cane floor. He was very glad to see Amma . . . but his disappointment that Arul wasn't here was deep. He ran his hand through his hair. Why didn't Amma tell him what was going on?

The sun began to slip below the palms and tamarind trees in the west, making the mountains in the distance stand out in purple silhouette.

The normal time for supper came and went, but no one gathered to eat. Instead, most of the girls and some of the *accals* wandered down toward the gate. A few of the girls climbed up on the gate and peered over.

The crowd at the gate got larger and larger. John got up from the porch and had just decided to go see what was happening when he heard a shout raised in Tamil, "They're coming! They're coming!"

Who's coming? John wondered. Just then Amy Carmichael and the others in the main house came running out. "Come, John!" Amy called, grabbing his hand and pulling him along. "You will want to see!"

Several of the older girls lit one torch from a cooking fire, then lit all the other torches. Soon a blaze of light danced in the twilight. Azim had swung open the gate and the flock of girls surged into the road outside.

At first John couldn't see anything. Then he saw a bandy coming slowly up the road. But . . . it wasn't an ordinary bandy. White lotus and jasmine flowers had been woven all over the curved straw roof. The oxen that pulled the bandy had brightly painted horns and flowers tucked in their bridles and tied to the yoke.

A man and a woman dressed in white sat in the front of the bandy. All the girls were crowding around, jumping up and down, shouting, laughing, and throwing flowers.

John hung back and watched curiously as the bandy came closer. It looked like a wedding. The oxen stopped and the man leaped to the ground, then turned and helped the young woman to the ground. She was dressed in a snow-white sari, framing her heart-shaped face and large dark eyes. Amy reached them and gave the young couple a big hug, and there was much laughter. The next moment the young woman and man turned toward John, and a flash of recognition surged through his body.

It was Jewel and Arul!

The couple saw John at the same time.

"*Annachie!*" Jewel cried.

"John! My brother!" said Arul. And the three friends clasped one another in a big bear hug, with little children hugging their legs and others still throwing flowers into the air.

In a few moments, they were pulled apart by the excited children, and the bridal couple was escorted through the flaming torches toward the main house.

John was bursting with questions, but a grand celebration was in full swing. Grass mats were laid on the ground for people to sit on; bowls and bowls of food and sweets and fruits were brought out on the porch. As the bride and groom were given plates of food, the girls gathered into a choir and sang a gentle Indian love song, followed by several beautiful hymns in Tamil.

John sat on a grass mat and watched the festivities. Every now and then Arul looked his way and flashed a grin as if to say, "Soon, my brother. But right now, Jewel comes first."

Amy sat down beside him on the mat.

"You see, John, I always knew Jewel belonged to God, and that He had a new life for her. How we missed her, so far away in China! But we knew she was in God's hands. Then . . . one night I had a dream. In the dream I saw Arul and Jewel getting married. When I awoke, I could not shake the feeling that God had shown me His vision for Jewel. So I talked to Arul. As you know, it is not uncommon in India for marriages to be arranged. But I didn't want it to only be my plan. I wanted it to be God's plan. So I prayed that if this is what God wanted, both Jewel and Arul would feel in their hearts that this was right."

Amy glanced fondly at the couple, each with an adoring child in their laps.

"Letters went back and forth between Jewel and Arul. And soon they both agreed: yes, they believed God would have them marry. But, even though Jewel is now of age, it seemed better for Arul to go to meet Jewel and be married in Ceylon, and then return. Now there is no question of her uncle's claim on her."

John nodded. Yes, it was right. He had never thought of it, because six years ago Jewel had still seemed like a child. But now she was a young woman of twenty. Who better for her husband than his dear friend and brother, Arul?

Amy touched his hand. "John? I have another dream. I have spoken of it to you before. There are so many boys, lost in the temples, sold to the traveling acting groups, abandoned by their poverty-stricken parents. They need Dohnavur, too. But we have been waiting for the men, men who can teach them. . . ."

John looked at Amy Carmichael.

"You have come back, John. You know the language. You are part of our family here. Will you ask God if this is why He brought you back to India? But I don't want it to be my idea. If it is God's idea, you will feel in your heart that it is right for you to do."

Just then several of the girls grabbed John's hands, pulled him up and led him in a merry chase of Follow the Leader behind the laughing bride and groom. Helplessly John looked over his shoulder at Amma and gave her a smile.

Yes, he would ask God about the boys. . . .

More About Amy Carmichael

AMY CARMICHAEL WAS BORN on December 16, 1867, in the seacoast village of Millisle in Northern Ireland. Her father, David Carmichael, and his brother William were respected mill-owners from a God-fearing family with a well-deserved reputation for integrity and generosity. The eldest of seven children, Amy was headstrong and full of mischief, but with a tender heart for all living things. It was a happy, secure childhood.

When Amy entered her teen years, she went away to a Wesleyan Methodist boarding school in Harrogate, Yorkshire, for three years. While away from home, the vital truths from the Bible that she learned at her mother's knee took root in her heart and she opened her life to Jesus as her Savior and Lord.

But things were not well at home. Financial diffi-culties took the family to Belfast and Amy had to return home from school. The strain on her father may have contributed to the pneumonia that took his life in 1885; Amy was only seventeen years old.

For the next several years she helped care for her younger brothers and sisters, and at the same time began holding Sunday classes for the "shawlies"— the girls who worked in the mills and wore shawls instead of hats. These meetings soon grew to such numbers that Amy decided they needed a building. In faith she prayed for five hundred pounds to put up an "iron hall" that would hold five hundred girls. Her faith and vision were contagious, and soon the mill-girls were meeting in a new hall named "The Wel-come," where they met for Bible study, singing and band practice, night school, sewing club, mothers meeting, as well as a monthly Gospel meeting open to everyone.

Amy's experience at "The Welcome" helped estab-lish many spiritual principles that she followed throughout her life, such as looking to God alone for financial needs and receiving help in her ministry only from God's people.

At age twenty, Amy was invited to England in 1888 to begin a similar work for factory girls in Ancoats, Manchester, and moved there with her mother and a sister. In England she met Robert Wilson, one of the founders of the "Keswick Conven-tion for the deepening of spiritual life." Attending her first Keswick convention at Wilson's invitation,

Amy committed her whole life to God. Wilson became a great friend of the whole Carmichael family, who always referred to him as the Dear Old Man ("D.O.M." for short). When illness and overwork forced Amy to quit her work in Manchester, she accepted Wilson's invitation in 1890 to come to his home, Broughton Grange, as a daughter and companion.

Amy thought God's plan was for her to care for the D.O.M. until his heavenly home-going—but on January 13, 1892, she heard God's unmistakable call to "Go ye" as a missionary and take the Gospel to foreign lands. Both Amy's mother and Robert Wilson released her to follow God's will, even though it was a great sacrifice for them.

But where was she called? Amy's missionary adventures took her first to Japan in April, 1893, but ill health forced her to return home a year later. No mission board would pass her for a foreign field; but, recommended by leaders of the Keswick Convention, she was accepted by the Church of England Zenana Missionary Society and sent to India in October, 1895. When she set foot on Indian soil, little did anyone know she would never return home again.

Amy threw herself into language study of Tamil so that she might share the Gospel directly with the people of south India. Her poor health took her to the hill-station of Ooty, where she met Reverend Thomas Walker and his wife, missionaries in the Tinnevelly District. Reverend Walker became her language coach, and as the relationship grew, the

Walkers invited Amy to join them in their evangelistic work in the Tinnevelly District. She called Walker *annachie* ("elder brother"); he called her *tungachie* ("younger sister").

With the Walkers' support, Amy gathered a band of Christian Indian women called the Starry Cluster who traveled from village to village in a bullock bandy, preaching the Gospel. One of these Indian women was Ponnammal, a young widow who became Amy's assistant until she died of cancer in 1915. Another young girl, Arulai, only eleven, was drawn by the love of God to this white woman in Indian dress. Arulai's boy cousin, Arul Dasan, also became a Christian in spite of persecution from his family. Both Arulai and Arul Dasan became valuable co-workers with Amy for many years to come.

It was while traveling with the Starry Cluster that Amy Carmichael first became aware of the "temple children," young girls who were "married to the gods" in the Hindu temples, a practice that included prostitution. Preena, age seven, was the first temple child to run away to Amy's protective arms in 1901. To provide a home for these girls, Amy established Dohnavur Fellowship near the village of Dohnavur in the Tinnavelly District. Soon Amy Carmichael became *Amma* ("mother") to dozens of little girls.

But Amma's heart also ached for the boys, some sold into temple service, others sold to acting troupes that traveled from town to town—a life that made it nearly impossible for these boys to grow up good and pure. The first two boys arrived in 1918; when Godfrey Webb-Peploe arrived at Dohnavur Fellowship in 1926 to help with the boys' work, there were seventy to eighty boys already!

The work at Dohnavur Fellowship followed a spiritual pattern that grew out of the Word of God and Amy's heart, represented in the key words: *love, loyalty, unity,* and *service.* She believed that co-workers in the Gospel should first and foremost love one another. Amma asked no one to do anything that she herself was not prepared to do. All work was considered a service of joy and love to the Lord. All needs were taken to the Lord in prayer, looking to Him alone for their provision, rather than letting their needs be made known to others. No money was borrowed; no debts incurred. God's will was often tested by the precept: "As God provides."

In October 1931, at the age of sixty-four, Amma fell into a pit, breaking her leg. She never fully recovered, and spent the next twenty years confined to her room. Yet new leadership was being prepared: Godfrey and Murray Webb-Peploe on the "men's side," and May Powell to replace Arulai, who was ill, on the "women's side." But Amy Carmichael continued to impart her faith and vision to both the children, who loved to visit her, and her co-workers. She wrote thirteen books after her accident, in addition to updating her earlier books. These books capture many stories of the lives of boys and girls, men and women, whom God brought to Himself through the work of Dohnavur Fellowship.

Amy Carmichael died on January 18, 1951, and was buried in God's Garden. No stone marks her grave; she is with Jesus. But her spirit lives on in the work of Dohnavur Fellowship in south India, still going strong today.

For Further Reading

Carmichael, Amy, *Gold Cord: The Story of a Fellowship* (London: Society for Promoting Christian Knowledge, 1932).

Elliot, Elisabeth, *A Chance to Die: The Life and Legacy of Amy Carmichael* (Old Tappan, N.J.: Fleming H. Revell Company, 1987).

Houghton, Frank L., *Amy Carmichael of Dohnavur* (Fort Washington, Penn.: Christian Literature Crusade, 1979, 1985).